HARVESTING GHOSTS

The system is sick, the cure is deadly!

T. R. Richardson

Foreword: A Warning and a Record

By T.R. Richardson

This book contains fictionalized depictions of systemic harm, institutional betrayals, and medical misconduct. It is inspired by real patterns, survivor accounts, and documented failures in oversight. The content may be disturbing—because the truth often is.

This is not a memoir. It is not a literal account of any one case. It is a forensic mosaic: a fictionalized warning built from real grief, real silence, and real complicity.

I am aware that speaking out invites discomfort, denial, and backlash. Institutions may respond with deflection or attempts to discredit. That is part of the blueprint. It is why whistleblowers are buried under paperwork, policy, and PR. It is why families are left with questions no chart will ever answer.

This book has been legally reviewed, emotionally vetted, and structurally designed to protect survivors while exposing systems. It does not name real individuals or institutions directly. It does not make factual claims about any one entity. It makes a moral claim about the cost of silence.

This is not meant to exploit real survivors. It's meant to amplify us—to give our silence a louder voice.

If you are reading this and feel defensive, I invite you to ask: Why? If you are reading this and recognize yourself, your loved ones, or your story—I see you. I believe you. And I am not afraid to name what others won't.

To those who say the content is "too sensitive" or "too risky": I say it's too important to ignore. To those who fear institutional backlash: I say silence is not neutrality—it is complicity. To those who ask how I know what I know: I say read the pages. The patterns are there. The warnings are there. The evidence is there.

To anyone who tries to silence this book, pull it from shelves, or quiet its author—your reaction only verifies your proximity to the harm. If this book threatens you, ask yourself why.

Watch for the backlash. The deflection. The "Look here, not there" tactics. They're part of the pattern. They always are.

I am speaking about secrets in towns all over the United States and beyond—secrets that are hushed and never brought to light.

If you're holding this book, you're holding a mirror. What you see in it depends on what you've lived—and what you've ignored.

This book is not just a story. It is a warning. It is a record. And it will not be erased.

Harvesting **Ghost**s

Inspired by real events

the system is sick, the cure is deadly

By T.R. Richardson

"Built from silence and grief, this story speaks for those who were never meant to be heard."

"A forensic unraveling of institutional betrayal—layered, relentless, and impossible to ignore."

"In the tunnels beneath spectacle, truth waits like a ghost. This book gives it a voice."

Harvesting Ghosts
© 2025 by T.R. Richardson

All rights reserved. No part of this book may be reproduced, stored in a retrieval system, or transmitted in any form or by any means—electronic, mechanical, photocopying, recording, or otherwise—without prior written permission of the publisher, except in the case of brief quotations embodied in critical articles or reviews.

This is a work of fiction. Names, characters, places, and incidents are either products of the author's imagination or are used fictitiously. Any resemblance to actual persons, living or dead, events, or locales is entirely coincidental.

ISBN:9798274425247

Cover design by T.R. Richardson
Printed in the United States of America

www.TRRichardson.com

10 9 8 7 6 5 4 3 2 1
First Edition

Dedication

The night before my husband died, as I held his hand, he whispered— **"Don't let them get away with this."** This is part of my promise to him.

Table of contents

CHAPTER 1 - O.R.
CHAPTER 2 - SHADOWS
CHAPTER 3 - INTAKE
CHAPTER 4 - TELEHEALTH
CHAPTER 5 - INTERVIEWS
    DELANEY
    CRAWFORD
    EMILEE
CHAPTER 6 - WAITING
CHAPTER 7 - TRANSFER
CHAPTER 8 – INDUCED
CHAPTER 9 – COFFEE
    Segment 1: "Karen's Second Opinion"
CHAPTER 10 - PUNCTUATION
CHAPTER 11 - POISON
CHAPTER 12 – IT'S DIRTY
CHAPTER 13 — LOCKER 111
CHAPTER 14 — ROOM 223
CHAPTER 15 – RIDDLES
    Segment 2: "Derrick's Missing Pieces"
CHAPTER 16 – PUZZLE PIECES
CHAPTER 17 – COLLAB
CHAPTER 18 - DR. OFFICE
CHAPTER 19 – BREACH
CHAPTER 20 – MINUTES
CHAPTER 21 – TRACKER
CHAPTER 22 – SHELTER
CHAPTER 23 – SCOTTIE
    Segment 3: "Linda's Fog"
CHAPTER 24 - RECORDS
CHAPTER 25 – WIDOW X
CHAPTER 26 – ALVEREZ
CHAPTER 27 - "EXPOSE"
CHAPTER 28 - SET MATCH

CHAPTER 29 – GOING LIVE
CHAPTER 30 – "THE PRETTY ONES"
CHAPTER 31- THE DRAWING
CHAPTER–32 FM DIAL
CHAPTER 33 – THE FUNNEL
CHAPTER 34 - AND A – 1
CHAPTER 35 – HEADACHE
CHAPTER 36 - THE BODY IN 3A
CHAPTER 37 - THE HONOR WALK
CHAPTER 38 - CLASS ACTION
CHAPTER 39 – ASTROTURF
CHAPTER 40- THE WOODS
CHAPTER 41 - DEEP DIVE
CHAPTER 42 - THE TUNNELS
CHAPTER 43 – TAKEN
CHAPTER 44 – THE HUNT BEGINS
CHAPTER 45 – INFILTRATION
CHAPTER 46 – GODS HOUSE
CHAPTER 47 – CUFFS
CHAPTER 48 – FALLOUT
CHAPTER 49 - BONUS CHAPTER – THE TWIST
No More Silence
EXTRAS

CHAPTER 1 - O.R.

The operating room was white—too white. Not the soft, forgiving kind, but the kind that reflected every movement like a mirror. Stainless steel trays glinted under the surgical lights, casting long shadows across the polished epoxy floor.

No clutter. No chatter. Only the whir of machines and the rhythmic hiss of oxygen.

"BP's holding at 92 over 54," murmured the nurse, her voice low and clipped, without looking up.

"Push two of heparin. Prep the preservation solution," said the lead surgeon, already elbow-deep in sterile gloves. His tone was clinical, but the clock behind him ticked louder than his words.

A second nurse adjusted the ventilator settings. "O2 saturation's dropping—eighty-seven percent."

"Boost flow. We need perfusion optimal before extraction."

The body on the table was still. Tubes snaked from every angle —arterial lines, central lines, a catheter draining into a sealed bag. The skin had been scrubbed raw, antiseptic yellow staining the torso like war paint. A sterile drape covered the face. No one mentioned a name.

"Cold ischemia window starts in twenty," someone said. No one replied. They all knew.

The floor beneath them was spotless, but slick in places—saline, not blood. Blood was managed, contained. The suction canister burbled, a grotesque lullaby.

Overhead, the OR lights burned hot, but the space itself was kept chilly.

"Scalpel. Midline incision. Let's go." Gloved hands moved in practiced choreography. Retractors clicked. A rib spreader groaned. The heart monitor beeped steady, then flatlined.

No one flinched.

"Time of cardiac standstill: 03:23."

"Begin flush."

The perfusion solution wasn't just icy—it was chemically tuned to preserve hepatic viability. The nurse tracked flow rates like a sniper tracks wind speed. Every second mattered. Every cell had a price. The solution poured in, icy and clear. The nurse observed the flow rate, eyes flicking between the I.V. bag and the stopwatch. "We're good. Pressure's stable."

"We'll need the cooler prepped in five minutes."

Outside the OR, the hallway was quiet. No family. No waiting room. Just a clipboard on a hook and a red light above the door that read: Do Not Enter. Inside, the team moved like clockwork.

The surgeon's voice was steady, but his eyes tracked the time. "Clamp the aorta. We're past the threshold."

"Flush complete. Tissue perfusion looks clean." The nurse handed off instruments without being asked. She knew the order. Everyone did. There was no room for improvisation. No margin for delay.

The chamber smelled of antiseptic and plastic.

"Time of completion: **03:42**." The surgeon peeled off his gloves. "Notify transport. They're cleared for departure."

The nurse nodded, already dialing and logging the Wells Supply cooler's serial number, timestamp, and seal integrity. Three initials were required—surgeon, nurse, and transport tech. No deviations allowed.

Chain of custody wasn't just policy. It was protection. Or at least, the illusion of it.

The lights dimmed. The machines powered down. The silence returned.

CHAPTER 2 - SHADOWS

Bright neon lights lit up the Buckles, Missouri Boardwalk at night. Rain cascaded into a perfect glow on every corner of the street. Crowds moved like waves under strings of lights. Laughter rang out from a group of college guys near a three-story mural of Elvis.

Nestled deep in the Ozark Mountains, Buckles was surrounded by dense woods and winding ridgelines. The town's edges blurred into forest, and it wasn't unusual to see a deer or raccoon wander across the street mid-festival—wildlife drawn in by leftover funnel cake and the hum of human noise.

On the sidewalk, dancers in shiny choir robes kicked high into the air. Their hymnals spun under flashing phone cameras. Tourists posed with fire-breathers and acrobats with faces that lit up with excitement.

At a crosswalk, a man in a silly tuxedo sang on top of a bucket, with a little monkey sitting on his shoulder, his voice was drowned out by the crowd leaving a comedy show, still laughing and eating hot dogs. The air was thick with leftover heat and the aroma of fried food.

Just past the fancy theater doors, the mood changed. In a dark alley behind the lights, a group of homeless sat quietly on crates, surrounded by old bags. They didn't speak, trying not to draw attention.

A security guard walked by, shining his flashlight without stopping or saying a word. He didn't even look at them.

Marcus was tall and stocky, carrying the tension of someone always bracing for impact. His skin was deep brown, his jaw sharp, and his eyes—bright blue but dark and watchful—rarely blinking. He moved like a man who had grown accustomed to being underestimated, every gesture deliberate, every silence loaded.

He walked through the shadows, head down, moving carefully. An old oversized camouflage military jacket hung loose on his frame, one sleeve long hiding the metal joint at his knee.

The damp musk of the Ozarks—wet leaves, cedar bark, and the faint tang of river stone lingered in the air. A possum darted across the alley ahead, startled by the noise of the crowd. Cicadas buzzed in the trees overhead, their rhythm pulsing like a warning. Somewhere behind the neon, the woods pressed close—black walnut, sycamore, and dogwood tangled in the dark like they were listening.

A street musician played the harmonica and accordion nearby, the music soft and almost happy—but not quite. Marcus clenched his fist, trying to hide the pain. People glanced at his limp, then quickly looked away. The heat stuck to him, sweat running down his back. Every few steps, a jolt of agony shot through his leg.

There it was, the Trinity General Hospital sign glowing in the distance—bright, bleak, impossible to ignore. No one could miss the bright blue neon plus symbol affixed to a white, too white concrete square atop the buildings heliport.

Between him and that beacon was a whole world of distractions: dreams of joy in facades of obscurities. Marcus saw through it. He saw the shadows behind the show. This town at night was full of masks.

As he crossed the street a large tour bus drove past with "Connections in Christ" painted on the side.

He limped past a crowd cheering for a fire juggler. A teenager bumped into him and muttered, "Watch it, old man." Marcus kept walking, swallowing the taste of blood in his mouth. The crowd pressed in, making it hard to breathe.

Pain shooting through his hip, and kept going until he found a quiet spot under a blinking billboard that read:

TRINITY GENERAL HOSPITAL .

WE DON'T WAIT FOR HOPE.

WE SCHEDULE IT.

He stopped, leaning against the wall, breathing hard. From here, the noise faded. No sirens. No shouting. Just the vibration of the city trying to lay the kids down for bed.

Three deer stepped into the street, hooves clicking on the asphalt. They moved slow, deliberate, like they'd done this before, seasonal migration. Their ribs showed through patchy fur, eyes glassy in the glow of the billboard. One turned its head toward him, unafraid.

They looked like **ghosts**—like something the city had forgotten but couldn't quite erase.

A truck labeled on the side "Wells Supply - Your Trust. His Glory. Our Delivery" whizzed by interrupting their calm and hurrying them away back into the dark back into the shadows.

The smell of barbecue hung in the air—smoky pork tangled with car exhaust and the sweet, greasy scent of fried dough drifting from the fairground two blocks down. It was the kind of scent that made you hungry and sick at the same time.

He whispered, "Even the wild things know where not to linger."

Marcus leaned against a chilly metal door, trying to steady his breath. The lock dug into his back—an old keypad model, the same type they used in Kandahar for field med kits. He scanned it instinctively, fingers twitching like they remembered the rhythm of bypass. He'd cracked worse with a paperclip and a prayer.

In the field, he'd built signal jammers from busted radios and detonated breaches with fertilizer and timing pins pulled from wristwatches. He knew how pressure moved through pipe systems, how heat warped metal, how to make something break exactly when it needed to.

His leg screamed. He clenched his jaw and kept moving.

The Hospital's logo flickered above him, glowing bleak and blue.

Cars rolled by, a thin moon peeked through the clouds. Behind him, neon lights from the entertainment district now colored the puddles pink and copper.

The joint of his prosthetic leg rubbed painfully against his skin. He closed his eyes. The night sky lit by explosions. Sand filled his mouth. Screams echoed around him. A fellow soldier crawled nearby, covered in blood. Then came the sharp pain in his leg, the silence, and the hard, cold ground. He remembered the sound of helicopters, but not relief—just emptiness.

Marcus opened his eyes to a family crossing the street. The father, wearing a jacket with "Your Trust. His Glory" on the back, guided his son who looked to be in his twenties, as he walked slowly with crutches.

The boy's leg was wrapped in plastic. The mother stayed close, watching him close. Even though he now towered over her she still looked at him like a young boy in need of protection. She carried an aura she could protect him from everything. Marcus felt a deep ache inside as he watched them disappear heading toward the hospital.

He touched the tattoo hidden under his sleeve—a faded Brahma bull. It was old, inked before the war, before everything changed. He whispered, "Trust no one but yourself," half prayer, half warning. There was no backup now, no brothers-in-arms. Just him and his stubborn will to keep going.

Near the emergency entrance, paramedics loaded a woman into an ambulance. Her face was pale, her body shaking. "F99," one paramedic mutters. "No family contact. No insurance." The other nods. They slammed the ambulance doors shut.

A van pulled up to the curb. Marcus recognized it—government plates, dented fender. The driver guided a younger guy out of the passenger seat toward the entrance. It looked like his buddy but he couldn't be sure. Driver gave the guy a reassuring pat on the shoulder, then turned back to the driver's seat and drove away.

Marcus looked back one last time, unsure which side of the door was more dangerous. Then he stepped forward, and the cold hospital lights swallowed him whole.

CHAPTER 3 - INTAKE

Marcus stepped into the bright emergency room of Trinity General Hospital . The fluorescent lights buzzed overhead, bleaching the room into something cold and too clean, like a stage set scrubbed of life. A balding man in a Trinity General polo and khaki pants fumbled his pen, letting it clatter across the tile just as Marcus entered. The timing was too neat—

Marcus shifted right, narrowly avoiding a stumble that would have sent him sprawling. He caught the man's quick glance upward, a flicker of something sharper than embarrassment, before the moment dissolved into routine.

Shuffling toward the reception window, Marcus tugged his old coat tighter, its frayed hem brushing against the hidden metal joint in his leg. The prosthetic clicked with each step, a sound swallowed by the hum of machines and the low murmur of voices, but one he could never quite ignore. The waiting area was full of subdued noise—chairs creaking, a clock ticking, someone coughing.

The receptionist looked up with tired eyes, handed him a blue clipboard, and shut the glass window without a word.

Marcus's hand shook as he filled out the form. The questions were hard—insurance, family, things he didn't want to think about. He wrote down his sister's number from memory as he sat in the cracked plastic chair, clipboard balanced on his knee. The form looked standard—name, DOB, insurance, emergency contacts but, each question had a small number printed beside it. Barely definable. Not part of the question. Just… there.

Insurance provider:

- None (33)
- Medicaid/ VA (21)
- Private (5)

Emergency contacts:

- 0 (27)
- 1–2 (11)
- 3+ (0)

Blood type:

- O- (37)
- AB (18)
- A/B+ (10)
- Unknown (5)

Current address:

- Homeless (20)
- Shelter (13)
- Permanent (5))

Employment status:

- Unemployed (15)
- Disabled (17)
- Employed (0)

Marcus checked "VA" for insurance. "2" for contacts. "O-" for blood type. "Shelter" for address. "Disabled" for employment.

He paused. Did the numbers mean something?

He added them up in his head. 21+ 11 + 37 + 13 + 17 = 99.

He snorted. "Must mean I'm gonna party like it's 1999," he muttered. "Or there's 99 bottles of beer on the wall. Maybe 99 red balloons overhead."

He leaned back, trying to ignore the ache in his leg.

A guy and girl each with a cup of coffee in their hand walks by talking. One wore a badge that read "Billing Liaison." The other had scrubs and a clipboard.

Guy "…. That's a goldmine. You can bill for a lobotomy one day and cognitive therapy the next."

Girl "Like billing one guy for brain removal and then charging for his mental health screening. Same week."

Guy "keeps 'em alive just long enough to rack up the codes. Since COVID, VA pays out like it's Christmas." They both laughed as their voices trailed off.

A moth fluttered near the ceiling light, a toddler cried nearby, her mother trying to calm her. There was a whiff in the air of cleaning chemicals and burnt coffee from a broken vending machine. Marcus gazed at the drink choices, trying to breathe slowly.

A staffer pushed an old man in a wheelchair past him. Her scrubs were stained with spilled coffee. She snapped at the man to hold on tighter. She swiped a card to enter double doors.

An orderly dropped a pile of papers, and patient names scattered across the floor. Marcus recognized one— "Reynolds"—before the attendant scooped them up and rushed away. The name stuck with him.

A man in a rhinestone-studded white suit burst through the doors, clutching his chest like he was mid-performance—or mid-heart attack. His jet-black pompadour held firm despite the sweat, and his gold sunglasses slid down his nose as he gasped, before collapsing onto the floor. Nurses rushed to help him.

Meanwhile, a woman in worn clothes sat nearby. No clipboard, no ID, no one helping her. Her eyes met Marcus's, and he felt a sharp understanding—they were both invisible here.

Two security guards stood near the entrance with their hands in their pant pockets, watching the homeless patients closely.

In the war, he'd learned to read systems like terrain—watch for patterns, exploit blind spots. He wasn't just a soldier. He was a tactician. Trinity's security was sloppy, and Marcus knew why. The hospital bought the illusion of safety, relying on obvious symbols of order—the white rooms, the scrubbed antiseptic aroma, the metal trays—but the execution was broken.

He observed staff moving like machines, their eyes carefully avoiding contact. He logged the glaring flaws: the orderly dropping patient files, security guards lazily focused only on the homeless, the tired aide relying on a rigid card-swipe routine. The infrastructure was designed for optics, not genuine control, making its predictable flaws a visible blind spot to anyone trained to look for them.

A young volunteer offered Marcus a cup of water. He took it and nodded. The water had a metal fragrance.

Marcus lowered his head and waited, forgotten in a place meant to heal. A woman walked to the window. And asked "Will someone call me if she wakes up?" The intake clerk hesitated, then replied, "I'm not authorized to confirm patient consciousness without a signed release." The woman walked away sobbing.

He was finally called to a narrow hallway just past the emergency room doors. The intake clerk didn't look up. She typed with mechanical speed, her nails clicking against the keys.

A glass partition separated her from the patients, like a zoo exhibit in reverse.

"Name?" "Marcus Dean Hayes." "Date of birth?" "March 3rd, 1981."

She didn't ask why he was there. Just typed. Her badge read "Trinity General Hospital Excellence Through Order." Marcus studied the slogan, wondering who believed it.

A man groaned nearby, clutching his stomach. No one moved. A woman with a swollen eye wearing a rhinestone studded dress and long red silk gloves leaned against the wall, whispering to herself.

Bleach and old sweat encased your senses.

Marcus handed over his clipboard. The clerk glanced at it, added up the numbers, and wrote 99 and put a circle around it at the top of the page, then slid it into a bin without comment.

"You'll be called when there's availability."

He knew enough that if they admitted him now a discharge required vitals, psych clearance, and a signed release, yet he had seen patients wheeled out with half-filled charts. The establishment didn't heal—it cleared space.

He shuffled back to a plastic chair and sat. The pain in his leg pulsed like a warning.

A large, slow-moving orderly with the build of someone who'd spent his life lifting things no one else wanted to touch, with thick shoulders and a neck nearly swallowed by muscle, was pushing a cart of different sized boxes marked Wells Supply. He didn't look at anyone.

Marcus watched as patients were called one by one. A teenager with a broken wrist. A man with chest pain. A woman sobbing into her coat. He wasn't called. Marcus leaned back, staring at the ceiling tiles. One was stained brown. Another had a crack running through it like a fault line.

He remembered the war—how triage worked. Who got help. Who didn't. It felt the same here, just quieter.

Eventually, he was moved to a side hallway near the Delaney Wing, its name etched in gold above the entrance. The walls were cleaner here. The lighting softer.

"Here have some water," an attendant handed him a small white flimsy paper cup. He drank slowly, watching the staff move with precision. No one smiled. No one spoke unless necessary.

The janitor's hair clung to his scalp in careful lines, oiled and obedient, a ritual left over from better days mopped nearby, muttering under his breath.

"Convict a kid, collect the rent—Judge Delaney gets his sixty percent."

Then he went on singing

" He donates wings, he names the halls—then pockets cash from prison walls

..."You say what?"

he says to himself while feverishly mopping then repeats

"Convict a kid, collect the rent—Judge Delaney gets his sixty percent."

" He donates wings, he names the halls—then pockets cash from prison walls

Marcus got the very clear impression that the janitor was talking about the people in the paintings. There were rumblings around that the Delaney's had a financial interest in the land that the courthouse and jail were built on.

He looked at the portraits lining the wall—black robes, stern faces, courtroom sketches. Like sitting in a museum of fine art but more than pompous considering this was supposed to be a place of healing, Marcus thought of the irony, a painting of a judge and a lawyer, in a hospital …. "I thought there was separation between church and state paid employees," he chuckled to himself.

Then he recognized his old friend from the shelter—Tommy Reynolds, a man in his mid-thirties, weathered and frail—was being wheeled down the hallway on a gurney. His eyes were half-closed, face pale, in a hospital gown and socks with what looked to be a piece of paper sticking out of the top.

Reynolds. The name from the dropped chart. When he passed Marcus, they locked eyes for a brief second. Recognition. Tommy's lips parted slightly, like he wanted to speak, but the hefty orderly pushed the gurney faster.

Marcus sat up straighter, heart thudding. He almost called out—but didn't. The moment passed. The orderly pulled out a key card, swiped it, and Tommy disappeared through a set of double doors marked "Restricted Access."

A nurse passed behind Marcus, whispering to another, "Delaney's been watching the logs again. Must be audit season." The second nurse rolled her eyes. "She watches everything, like she owns the place." He shifted in his chair, pain shooting through his hip. He closed his eyes. He never met Delaney, but he could feel the Delaney presence—like a shadow behind the curtain.

CHAPTER 4 - TELEHEALTH

Rebecca Washman, late forties, looked every inch the debutante. Flawless makeup. Glossed hair. Teeth white, too white. Bordering on artificial. Long legs, a profound bust, and the kind of posture that suggested she'd trained with books balanced on her head.

She was a rags-to-riches story—if you counted the rags she wore as *Little Orphan Fannie* at The Lunch Box ten years ago. A strip club tucked off the highway between Buckles and Branson, the Bible Belt's dirty little secret. Back then, she wore glitter and desperation. Now she wore Chanel.

She stepped off the elevator at Trinity General Hospital , heels clicking. The Harrow Wing. Named after Marlin Harrow, a former board member and physician. The third floor was a study in architectural whiplash—an old 1940s reception desk directly across from a gleaming glass corridor. Un-cohesive. Jarring.

She wasn't supposed to be here.

She was supposed to be in the lobby, waiting for the PR liaison who never showed but, the signal was stronger on the third floor, and she needed to send her segment pitch before Channel 3's producer moved on to another hospital .

She turned a corner—and stopped.

A man in a Trinity-branded collared shirt and light brown pants slipped into Room 221, the soft scuff of his loafers swallowed by the hum of the corridor lights. The door clicked shut, but in that instant, she noticed the one beside it—Room 223—stood ajar, its darkness like an invitation.

The detail lodged in her mind, too precise to be chance.

Inside, a nurse in lavender scrubs sat beside an elderly man in a hospital gown. A camera rolled. A green screen glowed behind them. On a nearby monitor, a **telehealth** consult looped—gentle voices, soft lighting, scripted compassion.

Rebecca stepped in, blinking.

"Sorry," she said. "I didn't know this room was in use."

Dr. Crawford turned from the monitor, calm as ever. "No worries," he paused. "We're filming a segment for our virtual care initiative. A little mercy on camera."

Rebecca smiled. "You mean the one Channel 3's been praising all week? That's you?"

He nodded. "Guilty. We're called to serve—even when the lights are on."

She stepped closer, scanning the setup. The nurse glanced at Crawford, uncertain. He gave a subtle nod.

"I don't believe we've met," Rebecca said. "I'm Channel 3's newest 6pm anchor. And this—this is perfect. I've been begging our producer for a regular health segment. You know—'Trinity Talks' or 'Care Corner.' Something digestible. Feel-good. This is exactly the kind of fluff piece that gets traction."

Crawford's expression didn't change, but something in his posture shifted—a quiet calculation.

"We'd be honored," he said. "The hospital's committed to transparency and patient dignity. Scripture says, 'Let your light so shine'—even through a lens."

Rebecca laughed, flattered. "I knew you were more than just a scalpel. You've got vision."

She turned to the monitor, watching the looped footage.

"This nurse—she's great. So warm. What's her name?"

"She's no longer with us," Crawford said. "Transferred but, her spirit remains. We all carry the work forward. *Go ye therefore, and teach.*"

Rebecca shrugged. "Still. The segment's gold. I could build a whole series around this. Weekly check-ins, patient stories, maybe even a live Q&A."

She looked at him, eyes gleaming. "You and me, Doc—we could make Trinity sparkle."

Crawford smiled faintly. "If it brings comfort to the weary, then let it shine. Even the smallest light can guide the lost."

Rebecca's phone buzzed. She glanced down, then back up.

"I should go," she said. "But I'd love to talk more. Maybe… off-camera?"

Crawford stepped forward, voice low. "My office is just upstairs."

She hesitated—then nodded.

"Lead the way."

CHAPTER 5 - INTERVIEWS

Sarah stepped off the elevator onto the top floor of Trinity General—the administrative wing. It was cooler here, quieter.

A TV plays in the waiting room. A cheerful female voice narrates over slow pans of neon-lit streets and smiling families.

"Welcome to Buckles, Missouri—so named, locals say, because it's the buckle of the Bible Belt. With a population just over 13,000, Buckles sits at the heart of Rockford County, drawing nearly a million visitors each year. From gospel glitz to patriotic pageantry, Buckles offers wholesome entertainment for the whole family. Whether you're coming from Tulsa, Little Rock, or Des Moines, you'll find something to believe in."

She walked toward the reception desk, her boots making a dull thud against the polished floor. Sarah Hart was lean and angular, with short auburn hair that curled just enough to look unruly when she was tired. Her gray-blue eyes were sharp, constantly scanning, calculating. She wore a white button-up shirt with the faintest glimpse of a pink tank top beneath, black utility pants, and combat boots. Her gun was visible on her hip. Her shoulders squared, chin lifted.

Above the desk a plaque read. A plaque above the desk read: "To whom much is given, even more is expected—from others."

The receptionist looked up, startled by the directness of her approach.

"You must be Ms. Hart—"

"Detective Hart," Sarah said, cutting in.

She'd learned early that in realms built by men, hesitation was permission. You didn't wait to be respected. You claimed it.

The girl blinked. "Yes, of course. Detective Hart."

"I'm here to meet with your Hospital Administrator Delaney and Doctor Crawford," she stated firmly.

A gentleman approached as she spoke. "Right this way," he said.

He led Sarah down the hall and opened the door to the conference room.

The hospital's conference room was bright and cold, with buzzing lights and walls covered in dull art—flags, plaques, and faded photos of Rockford's founding families. It looked neat and official. The kind of place meant to impress donors and deflect scrutiny.

Detective Sarah Hart laid some of her business cards on the table and wandered to the back of the room, stood at the bulletin board, and began reading an invitation posted:

"The Sovereign Life Institute Honors: A Luncheon Celebrating Leadership in Medicine... Honoring Dr. Patrick R. Crawford, whose unwavering commitment to precision, innovation, and community care has shaped the very heartbeat of Rockford County's medical excellence..."

She scanned the flier. Her eyes flicked to the names—Dr. Patrick R. Crawford, the Delaney Wing. The language was polished, excessive. A performance.

Sarah Hart had learned to read rooms before she could read books. Raised by a mother who taught self-defense and a father who taught silence, she knew how to spot danger in a handshake. She didn't trust institutions. She trusted her instinct.

She glanced back at the conference room door a woman entered.

DELANEY

Ms. Delaney walked in ahead of two nurses, her posture composed, her expression unreadable. She moved to the head of the long conference table without speaking. One nurse pulled out her chair.

She wore a tailored blazer, silk blouse, and pencil skirt. Her frame was angular, her movements deliberate. Her face bore the unmistakable stamp of her father—square jaw, heavy brow, a mouth that rarely smiled. She didn't seek approval. She enforced order.

"I'm Margaret Delaney, the Hospital Administrator," she said, scooting her chair forward.

CRAWFORD

Just then, Dr. Crawford entered like a man stepping into a pulpit, scanning for a seat.

"Apologies," he said, smoothing his coat. "I was detained in prayer with a family in crisis. Time has a way of bending when grief is in the room."

He was tall, broad-shouldered, with salt-and-pepper hair combed with reverence. His suit peeked from beneath his white medical jacket, deliberately immaculate. The collar of his shirt arched over the lapels—almost priestly. He dressed with authority. He dressed for absolution. His presence filled the room like incense—meant to sanctify, not soothe.

Sarah motioned for him to sit as she, stood up with her palms pressed firmly down on the table. He walked back and stood by the door.

"I'm Detective Hart and as I said when I called, I need answers about two missing people last seen at this facility—Marcus

Hayes and Tommy Reynolds. I need access to their intake and discharge documentation."

Crawford folded his hands. "Our team reviewed the files. There's nothing unusual."

Sarah kept her tone neutral. "Then I'd like to see those files."

Delaney offered a tight smile. "We'll need to check with legal before releasing anything directly."

Sarah (dryly): "Legal? Of course. Wouldn't want to accidentally release a document that proves everyone's alive and accounted for. I'll just wait by the fax machine like it's 1999 and hope the subpoena comes with a fruit basket."

She paused. "Fine. Then let's start simple. Who signed off on their discharge?"

Crawford leaned back. "I reviewed their charts."

Sarah: "And were they stable? … Or just stable enough to be someone else's problem?"

Delaney: "Mr. Reynolds was. Marcus Hayes was under observation."

Sarah: "Observation? Was there a psych evaluation, or did you just shake a Magic 8-Ball and hope for 'outlook good'?"

[Awkward silence.]

Sarah (tilting her head): "Let me guess—the psych evaluation is also checking with legal? Or is it buried in a filing cabinet labeled 'Ethics,' right next to the drawer marked 'Oops.'"

She leaned forward. "So, you're saying Mr. Reynolds was discharged?"

Crawford nodded once. "That was the plan."

Sarah: "Then there should be documentation. Discharge papers. Psych evaluation. Biometric logs. Family contact. Or do you prefer to discharge patients with a firm handshake and a vague sense of closure?"

Delaney: "Once again, Ms. Hart, we'll need to check with legal before releasing any documentation."

Sarah (without blinking): "It's Detective, Detective … Hart. And I'm not asking for the files. I'm asking why your perfectly compliant facility doesn't already have them available. Or is compliance just a decorative word you hang in the lobby?"

Crawford: "I reviewed what was available at the time. The patient was stable. All of our decisions were medically necessary and appropriate."

Sarah: "Appropriate based on what—a crystal ball or a signed release? Because from where I'm standing, your version of 'available' sounds a lot like 'conveniently missing.'"

Crawford folded his hands with ceremonial precision. "Ms.… I mean Detective, practicing medicine is a ritual of observation. There are quantifiable outcomes to every decision made in this hospital . I carry a heavy responsibility with every one of my patients."

Sarah: "Then you won't mind answering for the ones who, according to your own procedure, seem to have vanished into a quantifiable black hole. Or is that part of the ritual too?"

Crawford: "I assure you; I am not just a doctor. I am a steward of healing. 'My focus is absolute, for I have set my face like a flint.'"

Sarah (raising an eyebrow): "Did you just quote Isaiah 50:7 like it was your own TED Talk? Is scripture part of the discharge checklist now? Right after 'Vitals stable' and before 'Amen'?"

Crawford: "I quote truth where it applies."

Sarah: "Does it apply to Marcus Hayes, or are we just baptizing the paperwork?"

Crawford: "It applies to every soul entrusted to my care."

Delaney: "Who is saying these people disappeared? I'm sure our records are exemplary. If there are any gaps, it would be because a portion of the file is under review but, they were discharged—not missing."

Sarah (scoffing): "You're talking about records I have yet to see. That's not transparency—it's interpretive dance."

Delaney: "The attending physician would sign off on any discharge."

Sarah (snapping back to Crawford): "So you signed off without seeing the full file? You're working with a partial view but demanding full faith in your decisions. That's not medicine—it's improv."

Crawford: "I reviewed what was available and made determinations using a variety of factors—not just papers."

Delaney: "We don't micromanage every form. Nor do we micromanage our doctors."

Sarah: "You oversee the system, correct? Your system has more holes than Swiss cheese—and less nutritional value."

Delaney: "Paperwork delays happen."

Sarah turned to the nurses, noticing the second nurse twisting her hands in her lap.

"Did you see Mr. Reynolds after intake?"

Nurse: "I—I think he asked for a blanket. Maybe around midnight. I'm not sure." She glanced at Crawford, then at Delaney. Delaney's stare was cold, her lips pursed. The nurse shrank back.

Nurse: "Sorry. The shifts blur together. Paperwork gets backed up."

Sarah let the silence hang before writing down the name and shift. She felt the fear coagulating in the nurse's voice—and the pressure behind it.

EMILEE

Sarah surveyed the other nurse.

Emilee Vaughn was soft-featured and quiet-eyed, with chestnut hair pulled into a loose bun and scrubs that didn't seem to fit right. She had a gentle presence—slim, unobtrusive—but her gaze held a quiet intelligence.

"I remember Marcus Hayes," she said. "He had a limp. Looked exhausted. He was polite. Asked questions."

Sarah nodded. "Did he seem confused or agitated?"

"No. Just wary. Like he didn't trust the place." Emilee's answers felt real—not rehearsed.

Sarah wrote everything down.

Delaney shifted slightly, throwing a look like a spear at Emilee. Then she spoke in rehearsed legalese, her tone clipped and calculated—like someone who'd memorized the language of power but never earned it. She wielded policy like a shield, quoting regulations with the precision of someone desperate to sound smarter than she was.

"Of course, Nurse Vaughn is speaking from memory. We wouldn't want any impressions to be mistaken for official documentation."

Emilee blinked. "I just meant—he seemed alert. Not confused."

Delaney's gaze sharpened. She glanced at Crawford, who gave a small nod. Then she turned directly to both nurses.

"And we appreciate your dedication. Let's be careful not to speculate. Our records speak for themselves."

Emilee fell silent.

Sarah surveyed the exchange. Delaney's tone was calm, but her correction was unmistakable—reframing their words, reasserting control. It wasn't just about protocol. It was about power.

Delaney folded her hands and looked back at Sarah, her expression reset to polite professionalism.

"I need access to biometric logs, badge swipe data, surveillance timestamps," Sarah said.

"If you'd like to also review the intake logs, we'll need to check with legal," Delaney stated with firm control.

Sarah stood. "Then I'll check with the families."

Delaney didn't speak.

CHAPTER 6 - WAITING

After the interviews, Sarah stepped into the hospital's waiting area. Sunlight streamed through tall windows, lighting up the chairs and the quiet tension between them.

A TV in the background is showing animatronic Bible scenes, dinner theaters, and a putt-putt golf destination with a slow-motion shot of Jesus walking on water between courses. A vacation station narrator is saying "Buckles spans just 20 square miles, but it punches far above its weight. The town is a patchwork of wax museums, roadside miracles, and dinner theaters where Elvis closes with 'Amazing Grace.' It's Las Vegas with a halo—faith, family, and funnel cake."

Families members sat clutching coffee cups, watching the elevators like they were waiting for miracles.

Sarah approached a woman clutching her purse tightly. Her eyes were wild with worry. She jumped up and hugged Sarah.

"What did you find out?"

"They're being extremely vague," Sarah said. "Which isn't against the law—but it is concerning."

"My brother's been missing for days. I kept calling. No one called back," the woman said. "They promised to call."

"Shelby," Sarah said, her voice soft with familiarity. "I've known you and your family since I was a kid. Tommy and I go way back. I know he has PTSD. He gets confused. Are we sure this isn't just him going off on a bender?"

"Listen to this." Shelby sat back down, pulled out her phone, and started to play a voice message.

Sarah crouched beside her.

"Excuse me," came a voice behind Sarah. Cool. Controlled. Unmistakable.

Sarah turned.

Delaney stood just a few feet away, heels silent on the tile, hands folded like a school principal about to deliver a lecture on hallway decorum. Her expression was thin, her eyes sharp.

"These families are understandably upset," she said, addressing Sarah but looking past her. "This isn't the appropriate place for interviews."

Sarah stood "I'm not interviewing. I'm listening. Radical concept, I know."

Delaney's gaze flicked to the woman on the bench, then back to Sarah. "If they have concerns, they're welcome to speak with me directly. As administrator, I handle all patient inquiries."

Shelby looked down at her hands. Her voice shrank. "I already tried. You said you couldn't tell me anything."

Delaney's expression didn't falter, but her tone cooled further.

"As I've explained, in the absence of verified consent forms and chain-of-custody documentation, our disclosure parameters are strictly constrained. Trinity General operates under HIPAA compliance and internal risk mitigation protocols. Without appropriate clearance, I'm not authorized to release patient-specific data. It's hospital policy."

Sarah stepped slightly to the side—not blocking her, but not yielding either.

Sarah: "Policy doesn't explain why patients are disappearing, unless you've added vanishing acts to the standard discharge procedure."

Delaney's eyes narrowed. "Detective, I trust you'll respect our procedures. If you have further questions, I suggest you schedule a formal meeting."

Sarah raised an eyebrow. "A formal meeting? Should I bring a cake or just the subpoena?"

She left and Sarah, then turned back to Shelby, who was sitting on the bench.

"Don't give up," she said.

Shelby nodded, tears in her eyes.

An older man came from across the room holding a military jacket. He'd been standing there, watching the interaction.

"Detective?"

Sarah turned to him. "Mr. Hayes?"

"Marcus goes to church with me every Sunday. Every Sunday without fail since his mom passed last year. There's no doubt he's missing. An old military friend of his said he was here a few days ago—and then his trail goes quiet. I called the hospital four different times and was sent to four different voicemails. I finally came down here to get some answers, and I see his jacket in the waiting room."

He pointed to the jacket he was holding. The name HAYES was stitched across the breast pocket.

"Something isn't right," he said, voice cracking.

There was a pattern—calls ignored, missing paperwork, charts disappearing. Her notebook filled with notes and circles, a mess of contradictions.

She turned toward the counter.

"I just want to know where she is," a mother yelled, voice

hurried.

The clerk didn't flinch. "All I know is that procedure states that without a signed HIPAA release, we cannot disclose patient location."

"She's nineteen and schizophrenic, she doesn't sign things."

"Well, she is over eighteen, so we're limited in what we can share." The clerk's voice was smooth, rehearsed. Not cruel—just empty. "HIPAA clearly states that…"

Sarah interrupted her "HIPAA protects privacy, not silence, you're not protecting privacy. You're hiding negligence. Try again"

The clerk blinked. "I'm following procedure."

Sarah jabbed back, "And I'm following a trail of missing people. One of us should be worried that your procedure doubles as camouflage for incompetence."

The mother sobbed. The clerk stamped the form: **Handled**.

Sarah had seen this before—facilities that looked perfect on the outside but hid mistakes and silence inside. Trinity General sold the idea of care, but behind the scenes, it seemed people were vanishing and no one was keeping track.

She felt guilt. Years ago, a friend had disappeared. Her case was closed too quickly. Sarah had been chasing **ghost**s ever since—but never this many at once.

She closed her notebook and looked around.

"I need you all to go down to the station and file formal missing persons reports, okay?" she said to the families.

They nodded and began to leave.

Sarah walked toward the elevators, ready to dig deeper into Trinity General's silence.

CHAPTER 7 - TRANSFER

Buckles pulsed with gospel music and fried sugar. Choirs belted out praise from temporary stages, and families drifted between booths selling scripture-themed kettle corn and "Faith First" bumper stickers.

The streets were barricaded for the annual festival, and Trinity General's loading dock had become a blur of movement—ambulances, supply vans, and volunteers moving freely through the chaos.

Emilee Vaughn's shoes slapped the stairwell as she descended fast, heart pounding. She'd just seen the patient log—**F99**. No family contact. No insurance. Discharged at 6:42 a.m. but, the girl—nineteen, schizophrenic, terrified—had never been cleared for release.

She rounded the second-floor landing when a new nurse stepped into her path.

"Hey, sorry—quick question," the nurse said, holding a clipboard. "Do we scan the wristbands before or after the cooler's sealed?"

Emilee blinked. "What cooler?"

"The one for the transfer team. I'm shadowing Sung today."

Emilee's stomach dropped. "Later," she said, brushing past. "I need to check something."

Cut to the Van

Inside the white Wells Supply van parked at the dock, the girl lay strapped to a gurney. Her eyes twitched beneath half-closed lids. Her wrists were bruised from restraint. The IV line pulsed slowly.

Sung, the male CPN, leaned in calmly and injected a clear solution into the IV port. He didn't speak. He didn't flinch.

He placed a green sticker on the I.V. bag then stepped out of the van, shut the door, and tapped it three times—sharp, deliberate.

The van rolled forward into the crowd.

Another identical van pulled into its place.

Sung opened the rear doors. Empty. Clean. Ready.

Spencer passed in a hurry, clipboard in hand. "Transfer Window B—03:40 to 04:10," he snapped, not breaking stride.

Back to Emilee—

She burst through the stairwell door and onto the dock just as Spencer disappeared around the corner and the second van settled into place.

Sung turned, calm as ever.

Emilee slowed her pace, masking her breath. "Busy morning," she said lightly.

Sung nodded. "Festival always is."

She glanced into the van. Nothing. No patient. No cooler.

"Everything good?" she asked.

Sung smiled. "Handled."

Emilee nodded, forcing a smile. "Of course." Headed back inside heading for the break room.

Police started putting up additional traffic barriers preparing for the festival parade that always went right in front of the hospital.

A nurse flagged Emilee down in the hallway, holding up an I.V. bag.

"Hey—sorry, is this right?" she asked, pointing between the lot number on the bag and her clipboard.

Emilee glanced at it. "Yeah. That's just a smudge."

"Oh. Okay—thanks."

The nurse nodded and moved on. Emilee kept walking, but her eyes lingered on the bag a second longer than they should have.

Delany's assistant Spencer was sitting alone in the break room when Emilee walked in. The purr of the fridge was the only sound.

He nodded at her as if to say hi.

She nodded, unsure if he was expecting a reply.

He closed the folder in front of him, stood, and left without another word. The door clicked shut behind him. Emilee glanced at the table—nothing left but a coffee ring and a folded napkin with **2:23** Lyle SMH

"Smack my head, yeah, that tracks." She muttered, threw it in the trash as she moved toward the coffee station.

The coffee had gone cold. She glanced at the coffee canister, replaying the interview with Detective Hart in her head. She hadn't said anything wrong. Just the truth.

Marcus Hayes had been polite, alert, wary but, the moment she'd spoken, Ms. Delaney had shifted in her seat—smiling, but not kindly. Emilee could still feel the weight of that glance.

The door opened. She stepped in, heels silent on the tile, blazer crisp, expression unreadable. She didn't smile.

"Emilee," she said smoothly. "I wanted to follow up on your comments during the meeting."

Emilee straightened. "Yes?"

Delaney walked to the counter, poured herself water, then turned slowly. "You spoke with conviction. That's admirable, but we must be careful with language. Words like 'wary' or 'distrustful' can be misinterpreted, especially by outsiders."

Emilee nodded, unsure what to say.

"I'm sure you meant well," Delaney continued, voice calm and lawyerly. "But impressions aren't evidence. We rely on documentation. Records. Not feelings." She took a sip of water, then set the cup down with quiet precision.

"This Hospital has a reputation to uphold. My grandfather built the Delaney Wing to serve this community with dignity. My father prosecuted cases in Rockford County for twenty years. We don't traffic in speculation."

Emilee swallowed. "I understand."

Delaney stepped closer, her tone soft but firm. "Good. Let's keep things professional. If you notice anything unusual, bring it to me. Not to detectives. Not to reporters. To me"

Emilee sat frozen, heart pounding. The message was clear: speak carefully, or don't speak at all.

CHAPTER 8 – INDUCED

That evening Emilee Vaughn was grateful to pick up another shift, Lord knows she needed the money. Nurse Vaughn had always double-checked her meds. It was habit, instinct, survival. She'd been trained to verify every label, every dosage, every patient ID. She'd caught errors before—wrong vial, expired lot, a barcode that didn't scan. She knew how fast things could go wrong.

That night, everything matched. The label matched the chart. "Serial Number 02:2386470-5" The dosage was standard. The patient—Mr. Lyle, diabetic, post-op—was stable.

He'd joked about the hospital food, asked for extra ice, and thanked her for adjusting his blanket. Thirty minutes later, he was in a coma. No warning. No allergic reaction. Just a sudden crash—his vitals flatlining, alarms blaring, staff rushing in.

Emilee stood frozen as the crash cart rolled past her. a discarded cooler labeled 'Wells Supply' sat in the corner She'd administered the injection herself. He was smiling. How could this accident happen? She thought.

Now he wasn't moving and before Emilee could even process the shock, Ms. Delaney's assistant, Spencer, called her into the administrative conference room just after midnight.

She followed him into the room hearing the team in Lyle's room saying **D.N.R**..... She wondered if they were saying he had a Do

Not Resuscitate because she just had a conversation with Mr. Lyle about all he was looking forward to.

She put it out of her mind as she walked into the room.

Spencer promptly left. The blinds were drawn. Atmosphere was cold. A single lamp lit the table, casting long shadows across the walls. Dr. Crawford sat at the head of the table, sleeves rolled, tie loosened. She stood near the window, arms folded, her expression unreadable.

Crawford's tone was clinical. "The injectable was mislabeled. It happens." Delaney's voice was softer, almost maternal. "We're not going to report it. You're a good clinician, Nurse Vaughn. Mistakes happen."

Emilee's hands trembled. "But, I didn't—"

Delaney leaned in, her voice low and deliberate. "You did everything right, but if this goes to the board, they won't see it that way. You know how they treat staffers. One failure and you're done."

Crawford nodded, his voice calm. "Let us handle it. Quietly." It's our duty. The medical system is chaotic, so we need to create the order and purpose for lives that are otherwise lost.

Her mind raced—was it her fault? Had she missed something? The label matched. The chart matched. She'd followed protocol. Still, she nodded. She didn't know what else to do.

Delaney offered a thin smile. "Good. We'll take care of the paperwork."

Emilee left the room feeling like she'd been pardoned for a crime she didn't commit.

Spencer – Delaney's trusted assistant rushes past her as she walked toward the break room to clock out with a folder. With a slight smirk he hands it to Delaney. She scours the pages.

Her face lightened and relaxed. "The Petersen case," she announced. "The judge signed off. No appeal. No audit."

Crawford didn't look up. "The Lord appoints rulers. We simply guide their hand."

Delaney offered a thin smile.

The next couple days, Emilee couldn't stop replaying what she should've asked—questions left hanging, facts she'd let slide. Guilt clung to her like ants to sugar. So did the cover-up she unwillingly became a part of. She kept her head down. She ignored the warning signs: the vanished chart, the fake stroke diagnosis given to the family, the missing medication log. The note she found in the breakroom that seemed to predict Lyle's death.

She told herself it wasn't her place, but deep down, she knew better.

She wasn't the only one.

Three other clinicians had similar stories. Wrong meds. Sudden comas. No reports filed. No consequences—just hushed forgiveness and a subtle reminder: *You owe us.*

One nurse started drinking.

Another transferred out without a trace.

A third stopped speaking during rounds.

Emilee stayed. She smiled. She worked. She kept her mouth shut, but something inside her had shifted. She couldn't decide which was worse: that they had tricked her into accepting the catastrophic oversight, or that she had truly been an accomplice.

CHAPTER 9 – COFFEE

Rebecca adjusted the strap of her camisole as she perched on the edge of Dr. Crawford's desk, one leg crossed over the other, sipping espresso from a paper cup she hadn't paid for.

Crawford stood behind her, buttoning his shirt with clinical precision. No rush. No apology.

"You always leave before the coffee kicks in," he said.

Rebecca stared at a paper on his desk: **Cleaning Schedule – Room 223 – Do Not Disturb – 02:23** Circled in red.

She smirked, swirling the cup. "That's because I don't need caffeine to stay sharp. So, question—this telehealth footage. It's pre-recorded, isn't it? A friend of mine said if you loop virtual consults, you can bill insurance over and over. Same tape, different patients."

Crawford didn't flinch. "Interactive care doesn't reimburse. Loops do."

"Well," she said, standing, "you might want to inform your staff that you now offer telehealth consults. Just for transparency."

Her blazer was draped over the back of a chair, sunglasses already in hand. She moved like a woman who knew exactly how long she could linger before it became a liability but, this morning, she lingered a second longer.

"So, anyway…"

She reassembled herself—lipstick reapplied, hair fluffed, skirt smoothed. A pendant glinted as she fastened it to her lapel: a number 3 encased in a silver circle. Subtle. Deliberate.

Crawford stepped closer, voice low but deliberate. Then lower still—solemn as a preacher at a pulpit.

"The Parable of the Broken Vessel," he said. "The tongue is a serpent in the mouth, coiled and waiting. There was a girl once, bright as a lamp to her city. She heard a Word not meant for her, and she loosed it, thinking it harmless. From friend to neighbor to crowd, it spread—until the secret was no longer a whisper, but a shout in the square. And when dawn came, her bed was empty. They found her by the water, still and silent, a vessel shattered without a mark upon it. No hand struck her. No chain bound her. Yet the debt was paid. For those who walk in shadow know this truth: The first to speak the forbidden Word must bear its price."

He let the silence hang. Then added, almost gently: "Best not to mistake gossip for light, Rebecca. **Some stories are written in blood. And some in water.**"

She smiled, but it didn't reach her eyes. "Don't worry, silly. I don't even remember what we were talking about."

She turned, glancing over her shoulder. "You want to grab dinner tonight, call me before nine. After that, I'm booked."

Crawford didn't answer. He just stepped forward and kissed her cheek—not on the mouth—brief, practiced. Like punctuation.

Rebecca pulled away. Her lips curved. Her eyes stayed flat. "You're lucky I like punctuation."

She walked out, hips swaying, sunglasses on before she hit the hallway but, the moment she was out the door, the sway vanished.

Her hand trembled as she adjusted her sunglasses. Air stalled in her throat—just once—and she swallowed hard. The espresso was suddenly bitter in her throat.

Her heels slowed. Her posture dipped half an inch. Just enough to betray the weight behind her spine.

At the nurses' station, Spencer Holcomb Jr. was gathering up files for Ms. Delaney. He looked up, startled. Eyes flicking from the papers to Rebecca.

Spencer was short, middle-aged, balding. His comb-over clung to his scalp like a stubborn idea. Khaki pants. Loafers. A collared blue polo embroidered with the Trinity General Hospital monogram.

She winked. "Morning, sweetheart."

His smile came a beat late—like he'd been somewhere else in his head.

She stood at the elevator, staring at the glowing numbers. Thinking how different things might be—how much more clout she'd have in this industry—if her husband were someone like Crawford. Influential. Untouchable. A doctor with power and pedigree.

Instead, she had a reporter. Local paper. Good heart. Sharp mind but, no leverage. No access.

And in places like Trinity, access was everything.

She stepped into the elevator, compact in hand, reapplying her lipstick as the doors slid shut.

She didn't want to be afraid of Crawford but, fear had a gravity to it. And sometimes, it pulled her closer.

Crawford intercoms' the nurses' station, voice low and dry. "Make sure Channel 3 gets the footage from the fundraiser. And tell Delaney I want Rebecca on the next panel. She's good for optics."

Spencer nodded. "Yes sir. I'm already moving."

Crawford lingered by the window, watching the elevator light blink down the floors. No goodbye. No regret. Just routine.

But for a moment, his hand hovered over the espresso cup she'd left behind. Still warm.

☐ Segment 1: "Karen's Second Opinion"

[SFX: Low hum of static, soft piano chords fading in]

DJ (calm, unsettling): *Welcome back. You're tuned to The Wake-Up Frequency. And this… is Foulpractice. Where the charts don't match the symptoms. Where the signatures fade but the scars remain. Where medicine forgets its oath—and the silence speaks louder than the records.*

We have Karen on the line. Some stories don't come with closure. Karen's begins with a diagnosis. And ends with a question no one wants to answer.

KAREN (soft, deliberate): *They told me it was cancer. Stage two. Aggressive. I did the treatments. Radiation. Burns. Nausea. Pain that never left but, something felt… wrong. I kept asking for the scans. The labs. The proof. They said it was textbook. So, I went looking.*

Three states. Four specialists. And not one of them could find it. Not even a trace.

DJ (low): *So, what did the radiation attack?*

KAREN (pause): *That's the part no one wants to talk about. It was nothing. I didn't have cancer.*

DJ (shocked): *Then what was it?*

KAREN: *I was part of the herd of cash cows. A money maker.*

[SFX: Piano fades into static]

CHAPTER 10 - PUNCTUATION

Emilee hadn't slept since Mr. Lyle's coma. Delaney had ordered mandatory time off— "for emotional recalibration," she'd said—but rest was impossible.

Every time Emilee closed her eyes, she saw the flatline. Heard the silence in Crawford's office—the kind that didn't ask questions, didn't offer comfort, didn't even blink. A quiet that hung in the air, just sat there like static, heavy and sterile. It was a suffocating feeling like the air had been vacuumed out of the room.

She'd buried the guilt. Buried the questions but, they kept surfacing.

Back on shift, she moved like a **ghost** through the east wing, restocking supplies under the pulse of flickering fluorescent lights. Her badge clipped low, her hair pulled tight, her eyes scanning everything.

She was flipping through a clipboard marked "Transfer Clearance." And an entry stood out

Patient ID: Conrad, Melissa F99 Timestamp: 01:49 Discharge Status: Cleared

Sarah confused. That same patient was just in a restricted wing a little after 4:00. "That's impossible," she muttered to herself.

That's when she heard them—two orderlies by the med cart,

voices low but careless.

"New staffer on 3 North," one said. "Fresh out of training. Got assigned to that rare cardiac case—Maria Alvarez."

"Yeah, and that sepsis cocktail they put together is strong. Better hope the novice checks the flow rate."

Emilee froze. Sepsis cocktail? For a rare heart condition? That made no sense. She turned down the corridor, her sneakers silent on the waxed linoleum, and slipped into Maria's room.

The I.V. bag was already clipped to the pole. At first glance, it looked ordinary—clear fluid, standard label but, then she caught it: the lot code. **02:23**. **A colon** between the 2's.

Her breath caught. She'd seen that before—on Mr. Lyle's bag. She'd dismissed it as a smudge. She wouldn't make that mistake again.

She moved quickly. In the dispensary, she found another bag—same medication, same dosage—but the lot number was clean. Just digits. No **colon**.

She swapped them out without logging the change. No one would question it. No one ever had.

But this time, she needed proof.

She pulled two syringes, drew samples from both IV bags, and labeled them carefully—one from the hooked bag, one from the one she'd just removed. Her handwriting was tight, deliberate. She set the vials on the tray, then grabbed the old I.V. bag to stash it.

Just as she turned toward the supply closet, the door creaked open.

Emilee froze.

The young nurse stepped in, humming softly—gospel-tinged, familiar. *"He gives His angels charge over thee…"* Early twenties, badge still stiff from lamination, ponytail too tight. She looked nervous but eager, clutching a clipboard and a fresh pair of gloves.

"Hey," she said, smiling. "Sorry, didn't know anyone was in here."

Emilee straightened, IV bag still in hand. "Just inventorying," she said, voice light. She turned casually toward the supply cabinet, grabbed a box of gauze, and nudged the closet door open with her hip. She tucked the old IV bag behind a stack of 'Wells Supply' saline flushes and closed the door with a soft click.

"They're always short on 4x4s in this wing," she added, pretending to scan the shelf.

The nurse nodded, stepping toward the IV pole. The clean bag Emilee had hung was still clamped shut.

"You're here for Maria?" Emilee asked.

"Yeah. Cardiac case, right? They said she's stable now. Just need to start the antibiotics. Has her husband Ian been in here yet?"

Emilee's heart thudded. She kept her tone even. " I didn't see anyone. Make sure you check the flow rate before you hook it up."

The nurse paused, hand on the tubing. "Right. I was just about to—uh, what's the best way to double-check that?"

Emilee stepped closer, pointing to the roller clamp and the drip chamber. "You want a slow, steady drip. Not a flood. Especially with cardiac patients—too fast and you risk fluid overload. Too slow and the meds don't reach therapeutic levels."

The nurse nodded, absorbing every word. "Got it. Thanks. I'm still getting used to the pumps."

Emilee smiled, masking the adrenaline still buzzing under her skin. "You'll be fine. Just remember—flow rate isn't just about speed. It's about control."

The nurse smiled, grateful. "Bless you for that. I swear, the Lord sends help in the quietest ways."

She turned back to the IV pole, unclamped the line, and adjusted the dial.

Emilee stepped toward the door, gauze box in hand, ready to leave—

The nurse glanced over, still focused on the IV. "You always label your samples like that?"

The vials.

Still sitting on the tray.

Emilee's pulse spiked. "Like what?"

The nurse shrugged. "Just looked… extra careful. I like that."

Emilee smiled, tight. "Old habit."

She pivoted back, feigning a stretch. "Oops—almost forgot these," she said, scooping them up and slipping them into her pocket in one smooth motion.

She stepped into the hallway, heart pounding, didn't take another breath until she reached the stairwell.

CHAPTER 11 - POISON

Downstairs, the lab was quiet. Victor was finishing his shift, hunched over a microscope, earbuds in. He looked up when she entered, startled—then smiled, soft and crooked.

Victor was younger. Smart. Gentle. Always a little nervous around her, like he didn't know if she'd laugh or bite. He'd once brought her a coffee with her name spelled right, with two "e"s. No one ever did.

"Hey," he said, pulling out his earbuds. "You, okay?"

"I need a favor," she said, voice low. "Off the books."

She handed him the vials. He hesitated, eyes flicking to the labels, then back to her.

"Emilee, is this—?"

"Just run them. Please."

He nodded. No questions. Just trust.

She waited in the breakroom, staring at the poster on the wall

Trinity General Hospital

Organ Donation Protocol – Internal Staff Guidance *Updated per Administrative Oversight Committee*

All staff must adhere to the following procedures when managing potential donor cases:

- Verify DNR Status
  - Check for red armband or wristband.

- Confirm DNR in chart with physician signature.
  - Log time of death per standard protocol.
- Confirm Donation Eligibility
  - Review chart for donor registration or family consent.
  - If flagged for retrieval, notify Wells Supply dispatch.
  - Ensure cooler seal and chain-of-custody initials are recorded.
- Maintain Clinical Dignity
  - No alarms. No code calls.
  - Honor walk may be initiated if staffing permits.
  - Use ceremonial flag (white with blue flame) for transport.
- Documentation Review
  - If paperwork is incomplete or missing, do not interrupt process.
  - Continue with standard retrieval prep.
  - Notify Ms. Delaney immediately for administrative resolution.
- Protocol Clarification
  - In cases of documentation error, staff are reminded: "If the patient is already deceased, the paperwork is moot."
  - Proceed with dignity. Do not escalate.

Questions or concerns should be directed to Ms. Delaney's office. *"Excellence Through Order."*

. Her coffee was cold. Her hands wouldn't stop shaking.

Victor found her less than an hour later. He looked pale. Shaken.

"Emilee…" He sat beside her, voice barely above a whisper. "The one with the **colon**? It's laced with fentanyl. Concentration's off the charts. Even a small dose—Emilee, it could wipe out a city block."

He slid the folder across the table, eyes darting to the hallway. "This version won't last," he said quietly. "They overwrite everything. You know that."

Her stomach dropped. Mr. Lyle. Maria. The **colon** wasn't a smudge. It was a marker.

She jumped up out of her seat and headed to the sink she then pressed her palms to the counter, fighting the urge to be sick.

She hadn't failed. She hadn't imagined it.

The system was poisoning patients.

And she had just stopped it.

She opened her phone and created a new folder. She labeled it with a triangle emoji—Δ—the symbol for change.

Her phone buzzed. No caller ID. Just a message: *"Keep tracking. You're not alone."*

Who was this? Who was sending her messages? Why her?

She was done being complicit.

She was awake.

Emilee started documenting everything. Every shift, every chart, every whisper.

At the nurses' station, she flipped through intake records. Names were missing. Notes were vague. One file was signed by a nurse who hadn't worked at Trinity in months.

Stickers had appeared on patient charts—orange "R," green "G," purple "P." No one could explain them. She logged each one.

She kept her notes handwritten. Tucked into a pocket-sized spiral bound journal. She used abbreviations, symbols, and codes—just in case.

A younger nurse leaned in one night, voice hushed.

"You hear about Tommy Reynolds? Spencer was overheard saying he left against medical advice (AMA) but, I saw him in the hallway after that. He looked confused."

"Did you report it?" Emilee asked.

"I tried. Ms. Delaney said it was already **handled**."

Emilee's stomach twisted. "**Handled**." That word again. She felt sick. She had to walk away.

She passed the portraits in Delaney Hall—Delaney's grandfather in a black robe, her father in a suit, smiling like he knew something. Rockford County had been run by the Delaney dynasty for decades.

She remembered Delaney's voice during orientation: "This hospital has been in my family for generations. We uphold standards here. Not gossip."

Emilee kept walking.

She wasn't just documenting now.

She was preparing.

CHAPTER 12 – IT'S DIRTY

The blinds were half-closed, but the tension in the room was wide open.

Ed tossed a manila folder onto the desk between them. It landed with a slap, pages fanning out like a shrug.

"Rebecca," he said, "I can't keep airing puff pieces about ribbon cuttings and therapy dogs. I need meat. I need exclusives. I need to be first to know, not last to clap."

Rebecca crossed her legs, slow and deliberate. "That's what the audience wants. Comfort. Familiar faces. A little hope."

Ed leaned forward, elbows on the desk. "No. That's what *you* want. Because it's safe. Because it keeps you in good lighting and out of the mud."

She didn't blink. "I've built trust. That's not nothing."

He sighed. "You're good on camera, Rebecca but, pretty comes in a can.

(a pause)

Journalism? Journalism's ugly. It's dirty. If you're doing it right, it should make someone sweat."

She folded her arms. "So, what, you want me to start ambushing grieving families in the ER?"

"I want you to stop protecting the people we're supposed to be holding accountable. Trinity's got more sealed doors than a casino vault, and you're over here filming choir kids and coffee carts."

Rebecca's jaw tightened. "You think I don't know what's going on in that hospital?"

"I think you know *exactly* what's going on. And you're choosing not to look."

He stood, walked to the window, and pulled the blinds the rest of the way down.

"I'm bringing in someone new," he said. "Print background. Hungry. Name's **Eli Navarro**. He's got instincts. I want you to show him around."

Rebecca's stomach dropped, but her smile held. "Of course. Happy to."

Ed turned back to her. "You've had a good run but, if you want to keep that anchor chair, you're going to have to fight for it. With facts. Not eyelashes."

The door creaked open behind them.

In walked a young man—late twenties, maybe. Tall, lean, with the kind of posture that said he didn't need to prove anything yet, but would if pushed. His shirt was rolled at the sleeves; his press badge clipped to the collar like an afterthought. A leather-bound notebook peeked from his back pocket, and his eyes—dark, steady—took in the room like a crime scene.

"Rebecca," Ed said, too brightly. "Meet **Eli Navarro**—our new field hire. Just transferred in from Tulsa. Print background. Investigative edge. Thought you two should get acquainted."

Eli extended a hand. "Big fan," he said. "You've got presence."

Rebecca shook it, her smile practiced. "Presence is just posture and lighting. You'll learn."

Ed clapped Eli on the back. "Rebecca's going to show you around. Get you up to speed on how we handle hospital coverage. Trinity's been a goldmine for us lately."

Eli nodded. "Looking forward to it."

Ed's phone buzzed. He glanced at it, then at Rebecca. "Play nice."

He left, the door swinging shut behind him.

Rebecca turned to Eli, her smile still in place but her eyes sharpening. "So. Tulsa?"

Eli shrugged. "Too many silos. Not enough sunlight."

She gestured toward the hallway. "Come on. I'll give you the tour."

As they walked, her heels echoed against the tile. Eli's steps were silent. He didn't speak, just watched. Not the way men usually watched her—but like he was already writing.

She hated that.

She turned. "Come on. I'll show you the edit bay. That's where the magic happens."

They walked side by side down the hallway. Rebecca's heels clicked like punctuation. Eli's sneakers made no sound.

"So," she said again as if she never heard a word, "Tulsa, huh? What brings you to Buckles?"

"Opportunity," he said. "And a *vacancy*."

She glanced at him. He didn't elaborate.

They passed the green room. Rebecca gestured toward it. "That's where we keep the guests until they're camera-ready. We call it the aquarium."

Eli nodded. "You've been here a while, right?"

"Eight years," she said. "Started on weekends. Moved up."

"Impressive," he said. "Most anchors don't last that long in a market this size."

She stopped walking. "What's that supposed to mean?"

He smiled. "Just that turnover's high. You've got staying power."

She resumed walking. "I have range. I can do soft features, hard news, live hits, donor galas, breaking coverage. I don't rattle."

"Right," he said. "I saw your telehealth segment. The one with the nurse and the green screen?"

Rebecca's jaw tightened. "That was a hospital -provided package. We just cleaned it up for air."

"Sure," Eli said. "It looked… seamless. Almost too seamless."

They reached the edit bay. Rebecca opened the door.

Inside, a producer was scrubbing through footage—looped B-roll of a nurse nodding sympathetically at a patient who never blinked.

Eli leaned in. "That the same nurse from the last three segments?"

Rebecca didn't answer. She turned to the producer. "Can you give us a minute?"

The producer slipped out.

Eli folded his arms. "You ever ask why they keep giving us the same footage?"

Rebecca's voice was low. "You ever ask why they keep giving us access?"

He raised an eyebrow.

She stepped closer. "This isn't a newspaper, Eli. This is television. We don't chase stories. We curate them."

He didn't flinch. "You mean you protect the narrative."

"I mean we don't burn bridges we have to cross every week."

He nodded slowly. "So, when Trinity says jump, you ask what font to use in the chyron."

Rebecca's smile was tight. "You're not here to learn. You're here to replace me." Realizing she said that out loud.

Eli shrugged. "I'm here to report. If that makes someone replaceable, that's not on me."

She stepped back. "You want to make a name for yourself, I get it but, be careful. This town doesn't reward disruption. It buries it."

Eli looked at the paused frame on the monitor—, timestamp RM022316:28, the nurse's face frozen mid-nod.

"I think the truth's already buried," he said. "I'm just here to dig."

Rebecca's phone buzzed. A text from Crawford: **Panel confirmed. You're still the face. For now. Blood and Water. That's the difference.** She locked the screen without replying.

"Tour's over," she said. "You'll find your own way from here."

Eli didn't move. "Thanks for the transparency."

Rebecca walked out, heels sharp against the tile but, her hands were shaking.

Behind her, Eli stayed still, and pressed play, watching the monitor. The nurse kept nodding. The patient never blinked.

CHAPTER 13 — LOCKER 111

Emilee kept an eye on Delaney as she walked to her car from the fourth-floor window. The administrator was gone for the night. It was time. Back to the job of gathering info

She returned to the nurses' station and began again logging every medication error. She cross-referenced patient files against insurance status and family contact. Patterns emerged.

Marcus's intake form was stamped "**Handled**." But no one had touched his leg. No pain assessment. No emergency contact called.

She reviewed a patient flagged for "routine infection." Labs were clean. No fever. No cultures. Yet the record showed a full course of Levofloxacin – an antibiotic.

Another patient—mid-thirties, no diabetes history—was suddenly on insulin. No A1C. No glucose spikes. Just a billing code and a signature from a doctor Emilee had never met.

She checked the provider list. Virtual visits. Dozens of them.

But Trinity didn't offer **telehealth**. Not officially. Not ever.

Then came the worst one.

A patient marked "discharged AMA (against medical advice)." But Emilee had seen him fall. He was unconscious. The documentation had been changed. No incident report. Just a clean exit.

She pulled up Mr. Lyle's file. The medication list was wrong. He'd been on blood thinners. The chart said he wasn't. He'd had a reaction to morphine. The record said he'd never received it.

As Emilee sat alone at the nurses' station, the moan of the overhead lights blending with the soft whir of the printer. The shift had slowed, but her pulse hadn't. She wasn't charting. She was hunting.

Patient files spread across the desk like puzzle pieces. She flipped through them one by one—medication lists, discharge summaries, billing codes. She wasn't looking for typos. She was looking for patterns.

She kept combing through patient files, for hours. A tessellation started to emerge, on every altered note, every billing anomaly, three letters appeared in the margin: **S.M.H.** – Smack My Head she murmured out loud.

Something else caught her eye.

Most of the patients tied to those altered records—those with unexplained medication changes, phantom **telehealth** visits, sticker-coded files—had been assigned to Natalie Hayes.

She started to replay—Natalie Hayes, mid-shift, mid-call, then gone. No goodbye. No transfer paperwork. Just a voicemail from HR saying she'd "resigned voluntarily." But Natalie wasn't the type to vanish. She was sharp, steady, who'd once pulled her aside and whispered, *"Watch the meds. They don't match the symptoms."*

Natalie Hayes was the kind of nurse who triple-checked dosages and left handwritten notes for the night shift.

Emilee couldn't shake the feeling. Natalie hadn't left. She'd been removed.

She waited until the locker room cleared out—late night,

post-shift quiet. She was hit with the stench of sweat and bleach. Three stalls stood empty. The mirror was streaked with sanitizer.

A radio is on in the background "Trinity General Hospital is proud to partner with Grace Revival Tabernacle for the Faith in Action Health Fair! Come out for free blood pressure checks, flu shots, and wellness consultations. Because when faith and medicine work together, miracles happen. Trinity General—where healing meets hope."

Locker 111 sat at the end of the row. It used to be Natalie's.

Emilee crouched beside it, heart thudding. The lock was standard—cheap, rusted at the hinge. She pulled a flathead from her supply pouch, wedged it under the lip, and twisted.

The metal groaned. The latch gave.

Empty.

No badge. No notes. No trace of Natalie's meticulous handwriting.

But something was off.

The interior was too clean. Not just wiped down—scrubbed. Sanitized. Like someone wanted it to look untouched.

Emilee leaned in, scanning the metal. Her eyes caught a faint scratch near the hinge—thin, deliberate, like someone had pried something loose.

She ran her fingers along the edge. One screw sat crooked. The panel didn't sit flush.

She wedged her fingers under the lip and pulled.

The panel gave way with a soft click.

Behind it: a narrow cavity.

Inside, tucked deep in the hollow space, was a small stack of folded notes—creased, clipped together with a rusted paperclip. Emilee's lungs suddenly forgot what to do. She exhaled then she pulled the papers free, hands trembling.

Handwritten charts. Medication lists. Billing codes. Patient names she recognized. And in the margins, over and over: **S.M.H.**

Her pulse hammered. She heard laughter outside the doors—too close, too careless. Panic rising, she darted into the bathroom stall, bolted the door, and sat down hard, the papers spread across her lap.

One note read: "The problem isn't the money. It's the God complex. He quotes scripture during rounds. Says the vulnerable are 'gifts to the waiting.' He genuinely thinks this is a religious mission." Another scrawl beneath it: "Everything leads back to the Bible and the passages."

Her throat tightened. The fluorescent light above buzzed, flickering like it might give her away.

Then—voices. Right outside. The locker room door creaked.

"All of a sudden she heard people in the locker room talking about Locker 111."

She froze, leaning forward, ear pressed to the thin metal partition.

"What is that doing open like that?" one voice said. "Is it broken?" another asked. "Look inside here—" "Is someone else in here?"

The voices overlapped, urgent, suspicious.

Emilee clutched the papers tighter, every muscle locked. The stall door felt paper-thin, the gap at the bottom suddenly enormous. She held her breath, praying the sound of her heartbeat wasn't loud enough to give her away.

She heard them leave as she glanced down. Another note read

Not alone. Not all of them.

Emilee gazed at the page. Natalie had seen it. Natalie had tried to stop it.

Locker 111 wasn't just a clue. It was a warning.

CHAPTER 14 — ROOM 223

Just then, her phone buzzed.

Unknown number. No contact photo. No preview.

She hesitated, thumb hovering over the screen. Then tapped.

Message received:

Code Numbers mark the poisoned well,

Recall the sign you know too well.

Seek the book, the verse, the key—

Unlock the door, the lie, the fee **223**

Emilee stared at it, heart thudding. No punctuation. No sender. Just that strange, rhythmic message—like a riddle or a warning.

Her first instinct was to delete it but, her thumb didn't move.

"Numbers mark the poisoned well…" Her mind jumped to the I.V. bags. The lot codes. The **colon**. **02:23**. The same code that had been stamped on Mr. Lyle's bag. On Maria's. The ones laced with fentanyl.

Her stomach twisted.

"Recall the sign you know too well…" The **colon**. The stickers. The triangle folder on her phone. Was it a sign? A symbol? A warning?

"Seek the book, the verse, the key—" Book. Verse. Key.

Scripture? She repeated in her head again "the book, the verse"

She opened her Bible app, fingers fumbling. Typed in the numbers: **2:23**.

The screen loaded slowly. She froze mid-inhale.

2 Timothy **2:23**

"Don't have anything to do with foolish and stupid arguments, because you know they produce quarrels."

She blinked. Read it again.

Quarrels.

What did that have to do with poisoned I.V. bags?

She scrolled up. Read the surrounding verses. Nothing about medicine. Nothing about hospital s. Just warnings about false teachers, about avoiding pointless debates.

She almost closed the app.

Then the word hit her again.

Quarrels.

She couldn't remember the last time she'd heard it—until suddenly, she could.

A mandatory HR class. Workplace harassment and bullying. Two months ago. The instructor had been a retired nurse from Arkansas, soft-spoken, with a drawl that made everything sound like a bedtime story—even the warnings.

"Now when my kids start to *quarrel*," she'd said, smiling like it was a joke, "I don't take sides. I just separate 'em and make 'em clean something. So, when y'all wanna quarrel. Go clean sumpthin!"

Emilee had rolled her eyes at the time but, now…

Maybe that's it, she thought.

She backed out of the Bible app and opened her calendar. Scrolled back.

There it was. - Harrow Wing – Room **223** Mandatory: Workplace Conduct & Conflict Resolution

Her pulse kicked up. Emilee stared at the calendar entry—Room 223, the riddle wasn't random. It was pointing her somewhere specific.

She remembered the beige walls. The whiteboard. The faded poster: *"Conflict Resolution: Listen First."*

She remembered the instructor's voice, feathered and slow: *"Quarrels don't fix nothin'. They just make a mess."*

Emilee stared at the message again.

"Unlock the door, the lie, the fee."

She was done guessing. She grabbed her badge and moved fast, cutting through the east wing—past the vending machines, the framed photos of hospital donors, the atmosphere was saturated in bleach and mystery. Her footsteps echoed in the empty hallway.

She slowed as she passed Crawford, gave him a faint, awkward grin—then picked up her pace the moment his eyes moved on.

Crawford adjusted his cufflinks, then turned to Nurse Sung.

"Is the mercy loop prepped?" he asked quietly.

Sung nodded. "Green screen's lit. Patient's been coached."

Crawford gave a faint smile. "Good. Let's keep the optics warm, even if the line's cold."

He started down the hall in the direction Emilee had gone—but the elevator behind him dinged open.

Delaney held the elevator door, tablet in hand. "I need to show you something."

Without hesitation, Crawford pivoted and stepped inside. The doors slid shut behind him.

Down the corridor, Emilee reached the Harrow Wing. It was quiet at night. Too quiet.

She stood in front of the door to Conference Room **223**, the keypad blinking softly beside the handle. Not numbers—letters.

"Seek the book, the verse, the key…"

Her fingers hovered, her heart hammered.

She typed: K. E. Y.

A sharp beep rang out as if to yell WRONG

She flinched. The sound bounced down the empty hallway, louder than it should have been. Like the walls were listening.

She almost choked on her own nerves.

Footsteps.

A flashlight beam swept across the far wall.

Security.

One of the night guards rounded the corner, slow and casual. He spotted her standing there in the dark, one hand still near the keypad.

He smiled. Nodded.

He kept walking.

She waited—counted his steps until they faded. Waited longer, until the silence returned.

Then she tried again. This time she reads the whole code again

Code Numbers mark the poisoned well – the MEDS

Recall the sign you know too well – the **COLON**

Seek the book, the verse, the key - TIMOTHY

Unlock the door, the lie, the fee $2.23.

She looks around and focuses back on the key pad and types

T-I-M-O-T-H-Y

The keypad blinked green.

Click.

Her chest locked as it disengaged.

She pushed the door open and shut it quickly behind her.

Inside: a bland conference room. Long table. Whiteboard. A faded poster still taped to the wall: "Conflict Resolution: Listen First." Next to Starlight Baptist Church Presents Racemakers for Pacemakers Sponsored by Trinity General Hospital "Helping You Live Longer, One Beat at a Time"."

But something was off.

The carpet near the far wall was scuffed—uneven, like something heavy had been dragged across it again and again. Emilee narrowed her eyes.

She stepped closer, rubbing the sole of her shoe across the fibers. The texture was different here—thinner, worn down. Like pressure had been applied in repetition. Maybe a trapdoor. Maybe a pressure plate.

She crouched, ran her fingers along the edge of the baseboard, searching for a seam. Nothing.

She stood again, pressing her foot down harder, shifting her weight from heel to toe. Still nothing.

"It's in the floor," she whispered. "It has to be."

She leaned against the wall to steady herself, one hand braced flat against the paneling.

Click.

She froze.

The sound was soft, mechanical—like a latch releasing.

She stepped back.

A seam appeared in the wall, thin and vertical, right where her palm had been.

Emilee stared.

Then, slowly, the panel swung open like a door.

Behind it: darkness. And the rustle of something alive.

She hadn't found the clue in the carpet.

She'd triggered it by accident.

Just like in the old detective movies she used to watch at her grandma's house—where mystery doors opened with a touch, and the truth was always hidden in plain sight.

Behind it- she couldn't believe what she was seeing, She snapped photos of everything and slipped back into the hallway.

Days earlier - Tommy Reynolds sat cross-legged on the vinyl floor, counting the stitches in the hem of his blanket. Thirty-two, thirty-three, thirty-four—then he'd lose track and start again. It calmed him. Gave him something to finish.

Outside his room, the hallway lights flickered. A low hum pulsed from the cooler unit down the hall. Someone had mopped recently—the air carried the aroma of lingering bleach.

Tommy reached for the drawing he'd made the day before. A dog with a crooked ear, sketched in pencil on the back of a discharge form. He folded it carefully and tucked it into his sock.

He didn't know why, but he wanted it close.

CHAPTER 15 – RIDDLES

A black limo pulled up to the curb outside Trinity General, its windows blacked out like sealed records. Delaney stepped out first, heels clicking against the pavement. She shut the door with a practiced flick.

The rear window rolled down halfway. Her father—former Rockford County prosecutor, now candidate for Rockford County judge—smiled from the shadows. A man who'd never lost a vote, only postponed accountability.

"Well," he said, voice smooth and sour, "still playing nurse to the paperwork, I see."

She didn't respond. Just turned toward the building.

Then paused.

"Oh—wait," she said, reaching into her bag. She handed him a slim folder, unmarked except for a single tab: *Mitchell Audit – Internal Only*.

He flipped it open, scanned the top page, and nodded.

"I'll make sure the audit doesn't reach committee," he said, starting to roll the window up.

It stopped midway. Rolled back down.

She turned.

"Just make sure the Mitchell boy doesn't wake up before the election."

She didn't flinch. Just turned and walked in.

She sees the janitor as she walks around the corner and hands him a clipboard and continues walking.

The janitor Grady stood by the closet holding the blue clipboard like it was something he'd just been awarded.

Grady was a middle-aged man with the posture of someone who'd spent his life hunched over mop handles and bad instructions. His frame was thick but uneven—shoulders broad, one hip tilted from a childhood injury no one had treated.

His skin was pale and blotchy, like he'd never left the fluorescent glow of the hospital basement. His eyes were small, deep-set, and always moving—never quite meeting yours, but always watching.

He wore the same faded janitor's uniform every day, stitched with a name tag that read "Grady" in crooked letters. The sleeves were too long; the cuffs stained with bleach and something darker.

He wore black boots. His left boot always came untied. His receding hair was slicked back in a way that said someone told him it looked good like that once.

He spoke in fragments—half-muttered warnings, strange rhymes, and phrases that sounded like they came from someone else's dream.

"She likes it when it's quiet," he'd say. Or, "The tunnels hum when they're full."

Most people ignored him.

Grady was a fifth-generation Buckles native, born into a family that had never left the county line. His brother-cousin Homer (who also worked at the hospital) was the only person he trusted, and even that trust was brittle.

There were whispers—about inbreeding, about mental slowness, about things that happened in the woods behind their childhood home. About them being born in and living in tunnels beneath the town.

Grady hunched over tying his left boot muttering to himself. "Don't let the rats out. Don't let the rats out. She said keep 'em quiet."

He stood up and slapped the side of his head, then laughed.

Spencer glanced at him and didn't hesitate.

He walked straight up, took the clipboard from Grady's hands. No words exchanged. Grady didn't resist. Just gave a crooked smile and kept walking.

The Spencer then turned toward the utility room.

The door was still ajar.

Inside, sharp bleach and cooler ice scraped his nose. The hum of the sublevel units vibrated through the walls. Spencer stepped in, scanning the papers on the blue clipboard—mostly pristine forms stacked flat but, one sheet stood out.

Creased. Folded once. A penciled drawing of a dog.

Crooked ear. Soft eyes.

Spencer stared at it for a moment. Then he it in one of the folders he placed with the clipboard on the middle shelf, behind a box labeled Wells Supply and a half-used roll of patient ID stickers as he was being summoned by Delaney from outside.

Her phone buzzed. Another burner number. Another riddle:

Code

The fever's false, the blood runs clean,

Yet charts insist on what's unseen.

Cultures empty, still they're fed—

The sticker shows the path instead.

Her reflection in the darkened window looked pale, hollow-eyed. She whispered the lines under her breath. *Fever's false. Blood runs clean. Cultures empty...*

She knew what it meant. Sepsis.

She immediately slipped into the records room. The buzz of the fluorescent lights pressed down on her as she pulled every patient file coded "sepsis" that week.

One by one, she flipped through them.

- No positive blood cultures.
- No elevated white counts.
- No fevers.

The charts insisted on infection, but the labs were clean.

Her stomach knotted.

She then walked the halls going in rooms and checking the I.V. bags hanging at each flagged patient's bedside to find s in the serial number.

That's when she detected the stickers.

Orange with a letter T. Green with a letter L. Purple with a letter N.

Each bag bore a small colored sticker, neat and deliberate, like part of an inventory system but, she'd never seen them used in any official protocol.

She leaned closer to one patient's bag. Orange sticker. The chart said "sepsis." The patient's vitals were stable, no fever, no infection.

Another patient: green sticker. Same story.

Her pulse quickened. The rhyme echoed in her head: *The sticker shows the path instead.*

Just then she had a thought about Maria's antibiotic I.V. she had switched out. She then ran to Maria's room. Grabbed her chart with authority – not caring right now if anyone caught her. The chart said sepsis but, the labs were clean. There it was, an orange sticker.

Emilee backed away, heart hammering. The "sepsis" diagnosis wasn't treatment—it was camouflage.

The stickers weren't random. They were the real markers.

She scribbled the colors into her notebook, her hand shaking. Orange. Green. Purple. She didn't know what they meant yet, but she knew one thing for certain:

The antibiotics weren't treatment. They were preservation.

Maria and the others weren't dying.

They were being prepared and sorted.

☐ Segment 2: "Derrick's Missing Pieces"

DJ (calm, clipped): *You're tuned to The Wake-Up Frequency. And this… is Foulpractice. Where the vitals look stable but the truth flatlines. Where the paperwork is pristine but the pain is persistent. Where the oath to heal is buried beneath billing codes— And the silence isn't accidental. It's engineered. We're on the air with Derrick. So, tell the listeners, you went in for a routine hernia repair?*

DERRICK (flat, restrained): *Yeah, they said it all went well but, I felt off. Like something was missing. They said it was normal. Post-op fatigue. Nerves but, it didn't feel like nerves.*

DJ: *So, you had additional tests?*

DERRICK: *Bloodwork. Scans. They kept saying everything looked* fine but, I knew my body. I knew something was gone.

DJ: Gone?

DERRICK: One kidney. Half a liver. Gone.

DJ (quiet): And the paperwork?

DERRICK: Clean. Too clean. No mention of complications. No consent forms. Just a signature I don't remember signing.

DJ (cold): Sometimes the absence of evidence… Is the loudest clue of all.

[SFX: Static crackles, then fades]

CHAPTER 16 – PUZZLE PIECES

The motel room smelled like stale coffee, synthetic citrus, and something chemical—carpet cleaner, maybe

Detective Sarah Hart sat cross-legged on the bed, surrounded by notes—handwritten names, intake dates, room numbers, fragments of testimony from families in the waiting room. scribbled in the margins of hospital pamphlets.

Her laptop blinked with half-finished emails. A legal pad lay open, covered in circles and arrows—patterns she couldn't yet prove but couldn't stop chasing.

Her hand hovered over a photo tucked beneath the pad. Her college roommate with that crooked smile.

"She was twenty," Sarah thought. "I missed the signs. I won't miss them again."

Outside, a neon sign buzzed. Inside, the silence pressed in like a verdict.

The TV was low in the background. Footage of Buckles faded into aerial shots of Branson. The narrator's tone shifted slightly, still friendly but competitive.

"Just across the river—and through the woods, as locals like to say—lies Branson, Buckles' older, flashier rival. The two towns have been locked in quiet competition for decades. Branson boasts bigger venues. Buckles counters with tighter values and curated moral spectacle. Billboard placement, tour bus routes, even gospel festival dates—it's all part of the game."

Sarah just got off the phone with several people who knew Margaret Agnus Eunice Delaney. The picture they painted wasn't flattering. Delaney had failed the bar exam three times. Then she cheated. Then she bribed. Then she impersonated. Her family bailed her out each time—not out of love, but out of legacy.

Her father, the newly elected Judge, following in his own father's footsteps, Harold Agnue Ennis Delaney III, had wanted a son. Her mother and baby brother died in childbirth. Her father never forgave her for surviving. The hospital job wasn't a promotion—it was a leash but, Delaney wore it like a crown.

Sarah flipped through the pages again.

Marcus Hayes. Tommy Reynolds. A nineteen-year-old named Lila with schizophrenia. A teenager with a rare blood disorder.

All admitted. All vanished.

She rubbed her eyes. The timeline didn't make sense. The records were incomplete. The stories were too similar.

She wrote down:

Dr. Patrick R. Crawford – plaque on wall: "To whom much is given, even more is expected—from others."

She finds a form filled out with the patient name and signers redacted it's a checklist that says:

Organ Retrieval Protocol - Trinity General Surgical Suite 3A
Procedure ID: 1025250323 |
Timestamp: **03:42** |
Status: Complete
Checklist:

- [x] Confirm patient vitals (BP ≥ 90/50)
- [x] Administer heparin (2 units I.V. push)
- [x] Prep preservation solution (Hepatic viability standard)
- [x] Adjust ventilator settings (Target O2 ≥ 88%)
- [x] Monitor perfusion pressure
- [x] Initiate cold ischemia window (T-minus 20 min)
- [x] Midline incision (Scalpel, retractors, rib spreader)
- [x] Cardiac standstill confirmed (Time: 03:23)
- [x] Begin flush (Perfusion solution, track flow rate)
- [x] Prep transport cooler (Seal integrity, serial log)
- [x] Clamp aorta
- [x] Confirm tissue perfusion
- [x] Log completion time (**03:42**)
- [x] Notify transport team
- [x] Record initials: Surgeon / Nurse / Transport Tech
- [x] Verify chain of custody compliance

Just then, a knock at the door.

CHAPTER 17 – COLLAB

Sarah tensed, then crossed the room and peered through the curtain.

Nurse Emilee Vaughn stood outside, soaked to the bone. Her hair was plastered to her face, her scrubs clinging to her frame. Rain poured in sheets behind her, bouncing off the pavement like static.

Sarah cracked the door. "How'd you find me?"

Emilee gave a half-shrug, blinking against the downpour. "It wasn't hard. You said you were just north of town, and this motel's the only one out here. You're the only car in the lot—and you're parked right in front of this door."

Sarah stared at her for a beat, then realized Emilee was still standing in the rain, explaining herself while getting drenched.

"Geez. Get in here."

Emilee stepped inside, dripping water onto the linoleum. Her scrubs clung to her frame, soaked through. Sarah grabbed a towel from the bathroom and tossed it to her.

"You're drenched."

"I know," Emilee said, wiping her face. "Didn't want to wait."

She reached into her bag and handed over a stack of papers.

"Notes and a timeline."

Sarah took them without a word, already moving. She cleared a corner of the bed, pushing aside her own notes and legal pad. The TV murmured in the background—Buckles versus Branson, gospel festivals and billboard wars—but Sarah was locked in.

"Names, dates, flagged blood types. I kept these off-grid. They match the pattern I listed in my notes."

She laid Emilee's papers out in rows, cross-referencing them with her own stacks. Names. Dates. Room numbers.

Sarah pulled out one of Natalie Hayes' hand drawn chart and became horrified. She had coded terminology categorized and defined:

CATEGORY - The Victim/ Donor

CODED TERMINOLOGY

Vessel/ Asset/ Inventory = The human being whose organs are being harvested.

Non-Protocol Yield = A victim who was targeted and murdered (outside official donation protocol).

Logistical Surplus = A vulnerable or missing person deemed easy to acquire without raising suspicion.

CATEGORY - The Organs

CODED TERMINOLOGY

Viable Assets/The Harvest = The organs (liver, kidneys, heart, etc.) that are ready for removal and sale.

Product/The Shipment - The final, packaged organs being prepared for transport.

CATEGORY- The Kill/Cause of Death

CODED TERMINOLOGY

Optimization/Terminal Event - The act of medically inducing death via overdose or lethal injection.

Assisted Expiration - Euphemism for murder under medical supervision.

CATEGORY The Processing

CODED TERMINOLOGY

Preservation Protocol - The specific methods (like administering antibiotics or flushing with cold solution) used to keep the organs viable.

Stabilization/Flushing - Administering drugs (like massive doses of Heparin/antibiotics) to prevent clotting and infection before removal.

CATEGORY- The Location/Transport

CODED TERMINOLOGY

Transfer Corridor/Sub-Level Access - The tunnels, maintenance areas, or secure routes used to move victims or organs covertly.

Extraction Point/Drop Site - The off-site location (like a warehouse or church) where the organs are removed or transferred to the buyer.

CATEGORY - The Documentation

CODED TERMINOLOGY

Vessel Disposition/Closure - Falsifying death certificates, discharge summaries, or other documents to erase the victim's existence.

Compliance Event/Scrub-The act of deleting or altering electronic records to cover the trail.

"Okay, where should we begin?"

Emilee was still toweling off, her voice low but steady. "They're targeting people. And they're using us to do it."

Sarah's fingers tightened around her pen.

"Us? You nurses? Why didn't you say something sooner?"

"Because I thought I killed someone—and they let me believe it."

Sarah looked up, her gaze holding.

Emilee pointed to a folded slip of paper in the stack she'd handed over. "These are more names. Patients flagged for transfer. No insurance. No family. All disappeared."

Sarah unfolded the note, then slid it into a second stack—one she'd labeled *Unverified but Consistent*. Her pulse quickened.

"Where did you get these?"

"I started logging after Mr. Lyle," Emilee said. Her voice faltered. "After they made me think I'd killed him."

Sarah looked up again. "You didn't?"

"No. I know that now."

Emilee tapped a column on a hand-drawn spreadsheet Sarah hadn't noticed yet. It was labeled *Internal Markers.*

"Every uninsured patient is coded F99. It's a psych placeholder."

"What is that?" Sarah asked.

"'Unspecified mental disorder.'"

"And that's a red flag?"

"Yes. It justifies polypharmacy—over-sedation, extended stays for 'testing,' or maybe even blood and plasma pulls. They bill for psych consults that never happen. I don't know—hell, they could be experimenting on these people."

Sarah flipped through her own intake logs. The F99 column was there—quiet, consistent, and damning.

"Then every F99 case disappears from the census within 72 hours."

Sarah nodded slowly, already scribbling.

Emilee hesitated, then added, "The patients are... sorted. I started noticing stickers—orange with a R, purple with a P, green with a G. They match the ones I found on I.V. bags and patient charts."

Sarah looked up. "Sorted how?"

Emilee swallowed. "I think there are two streams. The ones who go to the official donation centers—the ones with paperwork, consent forms, tracking numbers. And then there's the other group. The ones who go missing. Off the grid. No records. No follow-up. Just… gone."

Sarah's pen stopped moving.

"They're not just harvesting organs," Emilee said. "They're harvesting silence. And they're using the system to do it."

Emilee leaned over the bed, pointing to a name in Sarah's stack.

"Mr. Reynolds was moved late. I saw Homer pushing him. He looked scared."

Sarah looked up.

"Who's Homer?"

Emilee hesitated, her fingers tightening around the towel.

"He's… one of the orderlies," she said carefully. "Not on the official rotation, but he's always around. Night shifts, mostly. Doesn't talk much. Always reeks of spray paint. He just moves patients."

Sarah frowned.

"Moves them where? Or should I guess—wherever the scent of bleach and plausible deniability cling?"

"Usually toward the Delaney Wing. Or the sub-levels. Places we're not supposed to access without clearance. I think he's related to the janitor—Grady."

Sarah's eyebrows shot up.

"The guy who looks like evolution hit pause halfway through?"

Emilee smirked and nodded.

"When I was last there," Sarah continued, "that human glitch who moves like he's buffering in real life was standing in the middle of the hallway—like he was trying to wear a groove into the linoleum and summon something. Or like he was auditioning as a haunted Roomba."

Emilee blinked, then let out a startled laugh.

Sarah stood up abruptly, mimicking a stiff, slow shuffle across the motel carpet. Her arms dangled at her sides, her eyes crossed, her voice low and glassy.

"He comes up to me as I'm walking to the elevator," she said, fully committed now.

She hunched over, rocking slightly, her voice dropping into a garbled, cracked whisper.

"'She said you ask too many questions... you -smell – like - secrets.' "As she walks side-ways dragging one of her feet.

Emilee burst out laughing, covering her mouth with the towel.

Sarah straightened, grinning.

"I said, 'Tell *her* my secrets smell like warrants, and I brought an extra bottle for anyone still in a lab coat.'"

Emilee was laughing now, full-bodied and unguarded, the kind of laugh that hadn't had room to exist in weeks.

Sarah's voice started to break from trying to hold it in, but the more she tried not to laugh, the more her eyes watered and the giggles took over. Now every word came with a laugh behind it.

"So, I keep walking and get in the elevator, right? And before the doors shut, he comes up to the doors—" she leaned forward, eyes wide, "'The tunnels - hum when - they're full.'"

She threw up her hands. "Like what the…. I wanted to just throw a breath mint at him, but I said, 'Great. Let me know when they start singing show tunes—I'll bring popcorn.'"

They both cracked up, the sound bouncing off the motel walls like something sacred.

For a moment, it wasn't about evidence bags or missing patients or hidden wings. It was just two women, consumed and exhausted, laughing like they were at a sleepover, not unraveling a conspiracy.

Emilee, still catching her breath, leaned in and gasped.

"Well… I'm not sure he really knows how to tie his shoes and, well - he's Grady's brother cousin."

Sarah blinked.

"Brother cousin? – Shut the… Emilee, come on…. Brother Cousin?" The laughter heightened. "Is that the official Administrator Delaney's hospital designation, or just an unfortunate genetic shortcut?"

Emilee was still laughing.

"Yeah, you know—brother… maybe cousin, maybe both." She winked,

Sarah says "Yeah, why go across the street when you can just go down the hall"

They both laugh so hard they are crying

Trying to regain composure, Emilee wiped her eyes.

"I heard they live near the old maintenance tunnels," Emilee said, lowering her voice like she was telling a ghost story. "Some of the staff say they were born down there but, they definitely know every inch of that hospital . And Delaney keeps them close."

Sarah snorted. "Born in the tunnels? What is this, *Gotham General*?"

Emilee grinned. "I'm just saying, I've never seen them eat. Or blink."

Sarah leaned in, mock-serious. "Do they hiss when exposed to sunlight? Speak only in riddles? Wear matching coveralls and answer to names like 'Ratboy' and 'Socket'?"

Emilee laughed. "Honestly? Wouldn't surprise me."

Sarah crosses her eyes "If one of them starts quoting scripture while fixing a boiler with a bone saw, I'm out. I'll fake my own death and move to Oregon."

Sarah's laughter slowed, then stopped. Her voice dropped. "Back to Ole Admin Delaney? Close how?"

Emilee wiped the last of the laughter tears from her eyes. "She gives them tasks. Special ones. Off the books. And they always obey. Some have said those guys are her cousins."

Sarah threw her hands up "What the – are you freakin' kidding me? Well now that you mention it, if I put a wig on Grady and gave him a phonetic dictionary – yea I see it. Cousins. Raised by rats, fluorescent light and institutional dread."

Emilee chuckled. "Word on the floor is of them once fixed a broken elevator with a paperclip and a prayer."

Sarah leaned back. "How'd that prayer work out? I bet he also knows how to erase a patient file with a whistle and a wink."

Emilee nodded solemnly. "I'm not sure how many teeth he has, he is always whistling. And probably has a key to every door that doesn't officially exist."

Sarah poured them both a cup of coffee handed one to Emilee, then took a sip of her coffee. "I swear, if one of them pops out of a vent and offers me a tour, I'm quitting. I'll go sell candles in Branson and never look back."

Emilee laughed. "You'd last two days. Tops."

Sarah raised an eyebrow. "Two days? Please. I'd unionize the candle shop by lunch."

Sarah took a sip of her coffee. "Neither one of them better play the banjo, if so, oh Lord, I'm gone. I'll fake a seizure, bite a nurse, and get myself airlifted to literally anywhere with a functioning ethics board."

Emilee snorted. "You'd probably get billed for the bite."

Sarah pointed at the ceiling. "And they'd code it as 'spiritual aggression' and send me a pamphlet on healing through gratitude."

Emilee wiped her eyes again. "Honestly, I wouldn't be surprised if Grady's got a tunnel map tattooed on his back. Like a mole with clearance."

Sarah leaned in, mock-whispering. "I bet he sleeps standing up. In a janitor closet. Next to a mop named 'Justice.'"

Emilee lost it. "Stop. I can't breathe."

Sarah grinned. "I'm just saying—if Delaney ever needs someone disappeared, she doesn't call HR. She calls Grady and the Whistle Gang."

Emilee nodded bent over in laughter

Sarah took another sip "They show up with a cooler, a clipboard, and a smile that says 'Don't ask.'"

Sarah raised her coffee like a toast. "To institutional dread. May it always come with a keycard and a creepy cousin."

They toast and Sarah grabs a notebook off of the bed. "Well, I finally got a court order, they only gave me the intake logs – oh yea, and a masterclass in obstruction…with that said, I was able to check the metadata."

She flipped her notebook.

"Marcus and Tommy were admitted, but the records stop there. The intake log shows Reynolds admitted at 01:14. The entry wasn't created until 03:11. So either someone's lying, or the hospital runs on time travel."

"You said Marcus seemed wary. Did he say anything?"

"Just that he didn't trust the place. Said he'd seen things go wrong before."

Emilee hesitated, then pulled out her phone

"That is what I found in 'the conflict resolution room, Room **223**."

Sarah looked up. "The conflict resolution room?"

"From anyone else's perspective it's a conference room but, It's not just that."

Sarah looked intrigued

"There's a hidden door. Behind the wall. I triggered it by accident—leaned against the paneling while checking the carpet. It opened."

Sarah stared.

"Inside was a video studio. Green screen. Cameras. Monitors looping fake **telehealth** consults. Same three actors. Different wigs. Different gowns." she pulls out her phone and scrolls looking for pictures she took, 'Here', "

Sarah says "What the…."

They're not just killing them," Emilee whispered "They're profiting twice—once for the care they never gave…".

Sarah cuts in "and again for the bodies they take.

Long paused silence

"And that room was in the Harrow Wing"?

Emilee nodded

Sarah scribbled notes, her pen moving fast. "What's the Delaney Wing used for?"

Emilee glanced around, lowered her voice. "Technically? Observation and overflow but, Ms. Delaney watches it like a hawk. I truly believe they're targeting people."

Sarah looked up. "Targeting?"

Emilee nodded. "And they're using staff who don't even know they're complicit. They think they're following protocol but, they're doing the dirty work."

Sarah's jaw tightened. "They're following the protocol Delaney and her minions have preached. Following the procedures Delaney wrote. This is bigger than malpractice."

Emilee's eyes didn't blink. "It's a system."

Sarah leaned back, absorbing that. "A machine."

Emilee nodded again. "And we're the sorters. We decide who gets seen, who gets delayed, who gets disappeared."

Sarah stared at her. "You say that like it's normal."

Emilee's voice cracked. "It's not but, it's routine."

CHAPTER 18 - DR. OFFICE

There was no mistaking where you were when walking into Crawford's office. The air felt curated—like a chapel built for one.

Bookshelves lined the walls, filled with titles that didn't just suggest authority—they demanded it:

"The Divine Right of Leadership,"

"Chosen Vessels: The Burden of Spiritual Authority,"

"The Shepherd's Rod: Discipline and Dominion in Ministry,"

"God's Order: Why Some Must Lead."

Each spine gleamed like it had never been opened by anyone but him.

Another frame held a verse, paraphrased to suit the room: "The Lord disciplines those He loves—and so must we."

On the desk sat a leather-bound journal with gold embossing: "Sermons for a Nation in Decline." Beside it, a crystal paperweight shaped like a crown caught the light like a halo.

Rebecca Washman, Channel 3's news anchor, bent slowly to retrieve her black stiletto heels from beneath the desk. Her movements were deliberate, practiced—like she knew exactly how much space she occupied and how many eyes were watching.

She walked back across the office, leaned down, and kissed Dr. Crawford—ravagingly, slow. Then she stood, slipped on her heels, grabbed her purse, and slid on oversized sunglasses and a wide-brimmed hat. Her blazer was crisp, her skirt smooth. She stepped out legs first, like a woman exiting a limousine, not a hospital office.

She peeked back in through the doorframe.

"Thanks for breakfast."

Dr. Crawford followed her to the threshold, brushing her cheek with the back of his hand. His voice was low, commanding.

"Your pleasure."

He brushes the side of her cheek.

Rebecca had a sly smile

"The pleasure wasn't all mine," she giggled.

As she turned down the hallway, she passed Delaney.

"Margaret," Rebecca said, polite but cool.

"Rebecca," Delaney replied, equally measured.

They parted without slowing.

Rebecca stepped into the elevator, compact in hand, reapplying her lipstick with practiced ease. *Mrs. Rebecca Crawford*—now that rolled off the tongue. So much smoother than *Rebecca Washman*. The doors slid shut

Moments later, Delaney entered Crawford's office.

He was standing at the window, watching the parking lot below. Rebecca's car was parked near the edge, angled for a quick exit. The lot was filling with patients and staff. The morning light made everything look cleaner than it was—like bleach over blood.

Beyond the pavement, the tree line rippled in the wind—tall

pines and hickories swaying like a congregation. A pair of wild turkeys pecked at the edge of the lot, oblivious to the sirens and stretchers. A red-tailed hawk circled overhead, its shadow gliding across the roof of the Harrow Wing. Crawford's gaze lingered not on the people, but on the woods. They were always there. Watching. Absorbing.

He noticed the V.A. van from the shelter pulling away. The driver nodded to a nurse as she guided a patient inside. The man looked barely conscious, his wristband already in place. Crawford didn't flinch. He just stared.

Delaney entered without knocking, holding a coffee she didn't offer him. She walked to the window beside him, scanning the lot.

"He's early," she said, nodding toward the van. "I wasn't expecting that batch until noon."

Crawford turned from the glass. "And the paperwork?"

She dropped a folder on his desk. "I'm handling it. As always."

She began flipping through a slim folder marked *Wells Supply – Monthly Reconciliation*. Her tone was clipped, her posture exact.

"Dr. Crawford," she said, eyes scanning the invoice summary, "why are we showing a 22% increase in cooler rotations and transfer kits this quarter?"

Crawford didn't look up. "Seasonal surge. The festival always spikes intake."

Delaney tapped the page. "These aren't intake kits. They're outbound. And several line items list 'non-standard destination codes.' That's not typical."

Crawford leaned back. "Overflow logistics. We've had to reroute through the warehouse more often."

She placed a small slip of paper on the desk and pointed to the handwriting: • *Wells Supply – Priority. Transfer Window B*

Crawford took a pen and wrote beneath it: *03:40 to 04:10*

Delaney tucked the paper into her jacket pocket and closed the folder slowly.

"Then I need a clean trail. Wells is charging us for unlogged units and duplicate serials. If we're going to keep this relationship stable, I need clarity before the audit window opens."

She slid the folder across the desk toward him.

"Make it clean, Patrick. Or make it disappear."

She shifted tone, trying to lighten the mood.

"Admissions are up twelve percent this quarter. We're running tighter than ever. The new intake protocol is working—we're ahead of projections, and compliance is stable."

Crawford didn't turn. "Of course it is. The flock responds to order. They always have."

Delaney hesitated. "There's been some noise. That detective Hart—she's poking around."

Crawford finally pivoted, calm but sharpened. "Let her. The Lord's work is never without opposition. And besides…" He gestured toward the journal. "Truth is not democratic. It is delivered."

Delaney nodded, but her eyes flicked to the crown.

Crawford sat slowly, folding his hands like a preacher preparing a sermon. "We are not managing a hospital . We are stewarding a generation. And some must be led—firmly."

He looked up, indulgent Delaney's thin facade widened, just slightly.. "You really should see the numbers. I could walk you through them over lunch if you like. Whenever is convenient. To go over projections. I know how much you value efficiency."

He paused. "I do."

She walked to the window and looked out. "This hospital has been in my family for generations. I know how to keep it clean. Quiet."

Crawford's gaze flicked to the folder, then back to her. "You've been... instrumental," he said slowly. "I don't know what I'd do without you."

Delaney smiled, just slightly. "Well," she said, "I'm glad you see that."

He leaned in closer, lowering his voice. "Let's keep things smooth. I trust you to handle the noise."

Delaney nodded, eyes bright.

The doctor glanced at the framed verse behind her, then added softly, "I'm not the author of confusion, but of peace... because the servant who knew his master's will and did not prepare... will be beaten with many blows."

Delaney didn't flinch. She just smiled—steady and sharp—then turned to leave.

Outside the office, Nurse Vaughn stood pretending to refill a supply cart. She hadn't meant to eavesdrop, but the door had been ajar—and the voices inside were too sharp to ignore.

Delaney passed her heading to the elevator. As she stepped in and pushed the button, a slip of paper fell from her pocket unnoticed. The doors shut.

Emilee glanced down at her phone—screen dimmed, voice memo already recording. Delaney's voice carried. She'd captured the stats. The dinner offer. Crawford's tone—flat, then suddenly warm. It wasn't real. She could hear it in his voice. He didn't want Margaret. He needed her.

Her stomach turned. Crawford was using her to keep things

quiet. The missing records weren't accidents—they were strategy.

She wheeled the cart away, pulse racing. A she saw the slip of paper that lay near the baseboard. She bent, read the handwriting: *Transfer Window B – 03:40 to 04:10*

As she turned the corner, she nearly collided with Dr. Crawford.

"Careful," he said, catching the edge of the cart with one hand. "You're always in motion, aren't you?"

Emilee jammed the paper in her pocket then forced a polite smile. "Just restocking. Trying to keep up."

The Doctor stepped closer—too close. His expensive cologne was sharp and invasive. His smile was a practiced charm, perfected for influence. "I've noticed you," he said, voice smooth. "Especially the extra shifts. That kind of dedication is rare, Nurse Vaughn. I see you're saving for something big."

Emilee stiffened, keeping her expression neutral. "Just trying to cover my costs, Doctor. You know how it is."

Crawford chuckled, low and indulgent. "Of course. It's a heavy burden, isn't it, carrying everything on your own?" He let the words hang in the air, a predatory quiet. "That handsome young man of yours. He must miss his mother's presence."

Emilee's blood ran cold. She knew he had read her file—all personnel files noted family. Her son, Leo, was four, and his current absence due to her brutal, interstate custody battle was the razor's edge of her life.

Her ex-husband had taken Leo out of state without authorization, forcing her into an uphill legal battle that consumed every extra cent she earned. She picked up double shifts just to pay the retainer for her attorney. She forced her pulse to slow, knowing she had to keep him talking.

"My private life is my own, Doctor," she stated carefully,

maintaining a neutral, almost submissive tone.

Crawford didn't flinch. He tilted his head, his eyes scanning her face like he was trying to read her thoughts. "Of course, but doesn't scripture say that a child needs both parents in unity? 'Train up a child in the way he should go,'" he murmured, quoting Proverbs 22:6. "It takes a unified home to fulfill God's order."

He stepped closer, voice dropping to a conspiratorial hush.

"The system is complicated, Emilee. Legal systems. Family systems. Sometimes, to get the order you need, you require assistance from someone who understands how these things work. Someone with influence."

He reached out and brushed a stray thread from her sleeve, fingers lingering longer than necessary.

"I think you see more than you let on," he added. "And I see a mother who needs her son home. Perhaps we can find a solution that helps us both."

Emilee nodded, her face composed, her pulse hammering against the sedative offer she knew he was making.

"I'll keep that in mind." She turned the cart and walked away, throat tight, steps steady.

From the far end of the hallway, Ms. Delaney stood near the elevator looking for something, watching everything. She'd seen Crawford lean in. Seen Emilee step back. Seen the smile he reserved for nothing else.

Delaney clenched her teeth. Her fingers curled around the folder she was holding.

"it's always the pretty ones"

," she muttered.

Her eyes narrowed. She turned sharply and walked toward her

office, heels clicking like gunfire.

CHAPTER 19 – BREACH

Ms. Delaney stood in the administrative suite, reviewing the overnight logs. A nurse had left the intake system unlocked. A clipboard was missing. Someone had accessed the east wing records after hours. She didn't speak; she didn't need to.

From the corner of the room, a television murmured:

"Tonight, we celebrate another milestone at Trinity General Hospital , where innovation meets compassion. From surgical breakthroughs to life-saving coordination, Rockford County continues to lead the way. I'm Rebecca Washman, and as always—thank you for trusting Channel 3."

Spencer hovered nearby, waiting for instructions.

"Run a full audit," She said. "Every wing. Every shift. I want names."

"Should we notify anyone?"

Delaney's thin facade was sharp. "Not yet. Let's keep this internal." She walked to the surveillance monitor and rewound the footage.

A figure moved through the hallway—coat pulled tight, head down. Not staff. Not a patient. She paused the video, zoomed in. "Find out who signed in last night," she said. "And check the visitor log for aliases."

Later that morning, Delaney met with Dr. Crawford in his office. She handed him a folder—neatly labeled, color-coded. "We've had a breach," she said. "Someone accessed restricted records."

The Doctor raised an eyebrow. "How serious?"

"Serious enough to warrant containment." He flipped through the pages. "Any idea who?" Delaney hesitated. "I have suspicions."

Crawford leaned back. "Muffle it. We don't need noise."

Delaney nodded. "I'll tighten access. Reassign shifts, and I'll speak with Vaughn." She paused, then added with a faint smile, "You remember what happened last time you got too fond of a staff member."

Crawford's expression didn't change, but his fingers stopped moving. Delaney continued, voice smooth. "She asked too many questions. Got too close to someone she shouldn't have. You were distracted, and we both know that didn't end well."

Crawford looked away, "That was years ago."

Delaney's smile sharpened. "Some lessons are worth remembering. I'd also beware of the news anchor, you could slip, she could benefit" He didn't respond but, his silence was acknowledgement.

After a long pause, he murmured—almost to himself— "Romans 13:2 He who rebels against authority rebels against what God has instituted"

Across the hall, Emilee noticed it immediately—her login credentials had changed. Her shift had been moved. Her access to certain files was restricted. The system didn't ask for a password reset. It simply denied her.

She tried again. Same result. The patient logs she'd reviewed last week were now locked behind administrative clearance. Hallway cameras were grayed out. Her badge still worked, but when she scanned into the west wing, where the discrepancies had started, the light blinked red.

She passed her in the hallway and smiled too sweetly. "We're just streamlining," she said. "Efficiency is everything." Her voice was syrupy, rehearsed. Emilee nodded, her pulse raced. She knew what this was. It wasn't about efficiency. It was about containment. She was being tracked. Every step felt heavier. The break room door creaked louder than usual. A nurse she'd worked with for years avoided eye contact. The supervisor who used to joke with her now logged her arrival time with a clipboard. Emilee kept her face neutral, her movements calm, but inside, her thoughts raced. They were closing ranks. She had crossed a line.

She opened her inbox. A message from IT flagged "unusual access patterns." Another from HR reminded her of confidentiality protocols. Neither mentioned her by name—but both were warnings. Then a memo entitled "Non-Essential Infrastructure Access and Utilization Policy (NIEAP)."

It read - "To maintain 100% compliance with operational metrics, transport of Non-Essential Patient Inventory (NEPI) to restricted Sub-Level Conduits will be managed by authorized maintenance personnel per Attachment A, thereby minimizing exposure risk and ensuring efficiency metrics are upheld."

Holy acronyms she thought, what did that all even mean she asked herself.

She deleted nothing. She printed nothing. She memorized everything. In the hallway mirror, she caught her own reflection—tired eyes, permanent scowl on her face, a woman walking a tightrope. She adjusted her badge and kept moving. They wanted her hushed.

CHAPTER 20 – MINUTES

Somewhere Beneath the Delaney Wing

[Scene opens in silence. Then: the low hum of fluorescent lights. A vent. A shadow. Someone listening.]

He sat in the dark, breath shallow. The concrete was cold. The air smelled like dust and bleach. In his hands: a flowchart. Purple. Black. Green. Orange. He traced the lines like veins.

Then—voices.

Low. Clipped. Coming through the vent like a confession.

SPENCER (Board Secretary): "What are you saying?"

HARROW (Legacy Member): "I'm saying we have the parade route this weekend to cover any extra movement. Gannon's construction company just finished the faster access tunnel—runs under the hospital through the morgue. No more overhead transfers."

SPENCER: "Confirmed. That cuts three minutes off the window."

HARROW: "Wells Supply has the extra bundles already placed at the warehouse. Alvarez seems to be straying—we need to make sure he doesn't."

JUDGE DELANEY (Board President): "I'll send Margaret. With a care package. He'll remember where his pension comes from."

SPENCER: "Understood. And congratulations, sir—on the election."

HARROW: "Your father would be proud. Same seat. Same silence."

SPENCER: "Now—what does MWOP need to purchase?"

TABOR (Procurement Liaison): "Mid-West Organ Procurement needs dual renal bundles, pediatric cardiac sets, and two gray-designation coolers. No billing tags. No burial codes."

SPENCER (typing): "MWOP request logged. Retrieval protocol pending."

JUDGE DELANEY: "Thank you, Spencer. It's nice to know all this money can still buy power."

[They laugh.]

Then— A chair scraped. Footsteps. A voice too close.

UNKNOWN VOICE: "Wait. Did you hear that?"

A shadow passed the frosted glass. The hallway light flickered. Someone scanned the corridor.

SPENCER (low): "There's no one here."

He didn't move. Not yet. Not until the hallway forgot he was ever there.

They weren't reacting to chaos. They were designing it— Buying it, And packaging it as Fun, Faith & Funnel Cakes.

CHAPTER 21 – TRACKER

The Delaney Wing was subdued after midnight. The lights dimmed to half-power, the halls whispering with the low throb of machinery and secrets. In her office, Ms. Delaney sat behind her desk, blazer crisp, fingers steepled beneath her chin.

Delaney's office was pristine and deliberate—glass shelves lined with awards; a wall of donor plaques polished to a mirror sheen. The lighting was soft but clinical, casting no shadows. A single orchid sat on the corner of her desk, too perfect to be real. There were no patient files in sight, no clutter, and no windows facing the hospital floor—only a frosted pane behind her desk that looked inward, not out. It wasn't a place for care. It was a place for control.

Grady stood in front of her, rocking slightly on his heels. Homer loomed behind him, silent, expression blank.

Delaney didn't look up right away. She was reviewing a file—Detective Sarah Hart's file. Intake logs, visitor records, a copy of her badge photo. She tapped the corner of the page with one manicured nail. "She's been asking questions," She said. "Too many."

Grady nodded eagerly. "She talks to Emilee. She writes things down."

Delaney finally looked up. "Did you put the tracker on her car?"

Homer blinked. "I forgot."

Grady stepped forward. "I did. I remembered. Under the back bumper. Like you said."

Delaney smiled with approval. "Good boy." Grady beamed. Homer shifted, uncomfortable.

"She needs a reminder," Delaney continued. "Something to slow her down. Something she'll remember."

Grady's breath quickened. "You want us to scare her?"

Delaney stood, walked around the desk, and placed a hand on Grady's shoulder. "Grady, tie your shoe!" As he sat in the chair and bent down to tie his left shoe.

"I want her unsettled. Not harmed. Not yet." She turned to Homer. "You'll take that van. Grady will handle the rest." Homer nodded slowly.

Delaney leaned in, her voice lace and acid. "Make it clean. No witnesses. No mistakes." She then sat on the corner of her desk, crossing her legs. Grady started quivering and smiling, slobber dripped from his chin as he reached to touch her leg. Delaney grabbed his hand before it reached her knee.

Spencer walked in and handed her a case and turned an left the room. Delaney gradually got up. She handed Grady the small case—unmarked, cold to the touch. Inside was a syringe. "Just a sedative: enough to disorient, not enough to kill stick it in her good, Grady, and you will be rewarded."

Grady clutched it like a gift. Delaney stepped back, her tone shifting to something colder. "If she talks to anyone else—if she leaks anything—you'll know what to do." Grady nodded, trembling with anticipation. Homer said nothing. Delaney returned to her desk, sat down, and opened another file. "Go," she said. Grady stood up from the chair, made a gesture as if he was saluting, turned around like a sea sick soldier and marched to the door. Homer followed, leaving without another word.

CHAPTER 22 – SHELTER

[RADIO STATIC, THEN A HOST'S VOICE—MID-CONVERSATION]

HOST: "—I mean, look at Buckles. You wanna clean up the streets? You become a tourist town. They've got it mastered."

CALLER 1 (male, upbeat): "Exactly. You bring in the gospel shows, the neon boardwalk, the Elvis competitions—suddenly the problem disappears. It's not cruel, it's smart."

CALLER 2 (female, sharp): "Smart? You think turning a town into a theme park solves homelessness?"

CALLER 1: "It solves visibility. You flood a place with church buses and funnel cake, and the undesirables fade out."

CALLER 2: "Or get removed. That's what you mean, isn't it? You make it easy to make people disappear."

HOST (chuckling nervously): "Let's not get conspiratorial—"

CALLER 2: "No, let's get honest. Buckles is perfect for it. All that foot traffic, all those out-of-towners—no one notices when someone goes missing. It's camouflage."

CALLER 1: "That's ridiculous."

CALLER 2: "Is it? Or is it just efficient?"

[STATIC FLARES—HOST CUTS TO COMMERCIAL]

Sarah turned the radio off and parked her unmarked car near the

Veteran's Shelter. The engine hummed for a moment before Hart turned it off. The talk radio show still on:

The building looked worn down—paint faded, steps smoothed by years of heavy boots. The shelter stood quietly, like it had seen too much.

Inside, the office was small and cluttered. Faded posters lined the walls. A volunteer offered her coffee; she declined. She was here for answers.

Roy stood near a vending machine smacking the side of it and putting more change in. He kept a keen eye on the news on the TV mounted above his head, which was muted but flashing headlines: "Charges Dropped in Rockford County Assault Case—Evidence Mishandled." Roy glanced at the screen, then looked away. "That kid was in here last month," he muttered. "Said he'd testify. Guess that didn't stick." His voice was rough; his look was tired. He chose his words slowly, like each one cost him something.

He looked up at Detective Hart. "You the one who called about Marcus?" she nodded.

"Gunny Hayes, well, Marcus, came by last week," Roy said. "Looked bad. Said something felt off."

Sarah jotted notes. Roy described Marcus's limp, his haunted look, how he kept glancing over his shoulder like someone was watching him.

Roy's voice dropped as they stepped away from the vending machines, the croon of the hallway swallowing their footsteps. "He didn't trust the facility," Roy said, gaze fixed on the linoleum. "Said they were hiding something."

Sarah tilted her head. "Marcus?"

Roy nodded. "He came here looking for his wife, Natalie. She was a nurse—worked nights in the Delaney Wing a few years back."

Sarah's brow furrowed. "I don't remember her."

"You wouldn't. She vanished." Roy leaned against the wall, arms crossed. "One night, she called him. Frantic. Said something was wrong. Told him to come get her. Said she couldn't talk, just—'get here now.'"

"What happened?"

"He got delayed. Traffic, construction, something stupid. By the time he got to Trinity, they told him she didn't work there anymore; said she'd quit days before."

Sarah blinked. "But she'd just called him."

"Exactly." Roy's jaw tightened. "her assistant handed him a plastic-sealed bag. Said it was the rest of her locker stuff: scrubs, badge, a few pens, and her cross necklace."

The ache reached Hart's ribs. "A cross?"

Roy nodded slowly. "Her mother's. She never took it off. Not even in surgery. Marcus used to joke it was her 'sterile miracle charm.'"

Sarah looked away. "So, they just gave it to him?"

"Like it meant nothing. Like she'd left it behind on purpose." Roy's voice cracked. "He went crazy after that: checked every hospital in the county, filed missing persons, slept in his car outside Trinity for weeks. Said he seen someone who looked like her once, in a lab coat, behind the glass—but they turned away before he could be sure."

"Did anyone investigate?"

Roy gave a bitter laugh. "They said she resigned voluntarily. No red flags. No incident report. Just… gone."

Sarah's voice was barely a whisper. "And Marcus?"

"He kept digging. Said the facility was covering something up.

Said Natalie seen something she wasn't supposed to. He started showing up at board meetings, handing out flyers. They called him unstable."

"Was he?"

Roy looked at her, his look hollow. "Wouldn't you be?"

Sarah asked about other veterans. Roy nodded. "Tommy Reynolds came here too. I was the one that gave him a ride to Trinity General—then he just disappeared." Sarah's stomach tightened. The blueprint was growing clearer—veterans going in, not coming out, and no one giving straight answers.

Sarah left the shelter with a list of names and dates, her notebook full of stories that didn't match the Hospital's records. Outside, the wind had picked up. Hart walked toward her car, flipping through her notes, her breath fogging in the cold air. She saw a note stuck to her windshield wiper it read "*The truth shall make you free.*" Overhead a billboard buzzed: CHANNEL 3 Rockford County's "most trusted source." *Then a* voice reached her from the alley.

"Detective Hart."

She turned. A man stood half in shadow, coat zipped high, eyes wary. "I watched you go in," he said. "Figured you'd show up eventually."

Sarah didn't speak right away. She lowered her notebook. "You've been watching the shelter?"

The man nodded. "It's the only place I trust." He glanced toward the street. "I didn't come to be found. I came to warn you."

Sarah stepped closer. "About Trinity General Hospital ?"

"About what they do to people who ask questions." His voice was low. "I saw what happened to Tommy. I know what they tried to do to me."

Sarah's grip tightened on her notebook. "Marcus? Is that you, Marcus? You need to tell me everything."

Hayes didn't answer. He looked past her, scanning the street like he was expecting someone—or avoiding someone. "I overheard a board meeting," he said. "But not here. Too many ears."

He turned and walked away, not looking back.

Sarah rushed to where he'd been standing. On the ground lay a color-coded flowchart—boxes marked in **Purple**, **Black**, **Green**, **Orange**—and a second page, handwritten. At the top, one line stood out: **Spencer – d assist.**

She glanced up. Marcus was already gone, swallowed by the dark.

Her pulse was steady but, rising.

She didn't have a victim. She had a witness.

CHAPTER 23 – SCOTTIE

Sarah sat in her car outside the shelter, notebook full, heart heavy. Marcus's words echoed in her mind—his distrust, his fear, the way he looked over his shoulder like danger had a name. She had what she needed to move forward, but she needed help. Someone who could make noise. Someone who still picked up when she called.

Hart scrolled through her contacts until she found him: Scott Washman. She hadn't said his name aloud in years, not since the wedding that never happened. Hundreds of guests. A cathedral full of flowers. His father, the former governor of Missouri, had arranged everything: press coverage, donors, a guest list that read like a political gala. Scott had waited at the altar for hours, tuxedo, just standing there at attention, eyes hollow, refusing to believe she wouldn't walk through the doors. She never did. Now he was married to the nightly news anchor Rebecca; they now had two kids. A house in the hills, but she knew how to reach him.

She typed: *Need to meet. Our spot. Tonight. It's important.* She didn't wait for a reply. She knew he'd come.

Scott Washman sat in his home office, the glow of his laptop casting shadows on the framed photos behind him—his wife, their two young kids, a family vacation in Destin. He stared at Sarah's message, heart pounding. He hadn't heard from her in years—not like this. His wife was asleep upstairs, and he knew if she found out, she'd lose her mind. She hated the name, the history, the way Scott still flinched when the wedding was mentioned but, he couldn't ignore the message. Not from Sarah. He grabbed his coat and keys, telling himself it was just a story. Just work. Just one meeting.

Beverly's diner sat on the edge of a quiet town south of Buckles, its neon sign flickering like a heartbeat. Inside, the booths were cracked vinyl, the coffee burnt, and the jukebox stuck on old country ballads. It was their spot—before everything fell apart.

Sarah sat in the corner booth, her notebook open beside a half-empty cup. She looked up as Scott walked in, his face was older, sharper, but still familiar. The reporter slid into the booth without a word.

"You look tired," she said.

"I have two kids," he replied. "And a wife who thinks I'm at the office."

Sarah nodded. "I wouldn't have called if it wasn't serious."

Scott leaned back, arms crossed. "You always say that."

She didn't flinch. "People are missing from Trinity General Hospital . Veterans. Patients. No release records. No movement. Just gone."

Scott's jaw tightened. "You're sure?"

"I have files. Interviews. A nurse inside. They're scrubbing records. Watching staff. It's happening now."

"These are Hospital records?" he asked.

"Some of them," Sarah said. "The rest are interviews, missing names, and proof that people were admitted but never discharged." He flipped through the pages, eyebrows rising. "This is serious."

Sarah leaned in, her voice barely above a whisper.

"It looks like they're preparing organs in live patients."

Scott froze. "What do you mean?"

Sarah's eyes didn't waver.

"Antibiotics without infection. It's not treatment—it's preparation. Broad-spectrum antibiotics are used to reduce bacterial load before harvesting. Keeps the organs clean."

She flipped a page.

"Insulin in non-diabetics. It stabilizes blood sugar, protects the pancreas. If you're not diabetic, it's not medicine—it's maintenance."

Scott's jaw tightened.

"Eye drops," she added. "Lubricants. Preservatives. Used to keep corneas viable. If you're sedated and getting hourly drops, it's not comfort—it's conditioning."

She pointed to a chart.

"Beta blockers. Vasodilators. They're used to optimize perfusion—make sure blood flow to the organs stays strong but, in patients who don't need them? It's not care. It's calibration."

Scott flipped through the pages again, slower now.

"If you have insurance," Sarah said, "you might stay alive longer but, your policy will be charged for tests that were never run, consults that never happened, visits that were never made."

She looked up.

"It's real. And it's happening now."

The reporter promised to dig deeper and publish the story. Sarah felt a mix of relief and fear. Once the truth was out, there'd be no going back.

He looked down at the table, then back at her. "You want me to run it."

"I need you to be ready but wait until I say go, or it could be devastating to everyone involved. We need to save as many as we can."

Scott hesitated. "Sarah… if this is real, they'll come after you. You know that, right?"

"I'm already in it."

The reporter rubbed his temples. "You always do this. You dive in, burn everything behind you, and expect me to follow."

She met his gaze. "You're the only one who'll tell it right."

Silence hung between them. The jukebox clicked. A waitress refilled Sarah's coffee without asking. Scott finally spoke. "I'll look at what you have, but I'm not promising anything."

Sarah nodded. "You always did have a thing for lost causes. I just never thought I'd be one of them." He stood to leave, then paused. "You broke me once. Don't ask me to watch you disappear too."

She didn't answer. She just watched him walk out into the night, coat pulled tight, heart still aching.

 Segment 3: "Linda's Fog"

DJ (somber, slow): *You're listening to The Wake-Up Frequency. Welcome to Foulpractice. Where symptoms are dismissed, and consent is a checkbox. Where the diagnosis is clean, but the damage is permanent. Where medicine wears a mask— And behind it, the system forgets who it's meant to serve. We're on air with Linda. She checked in with a cough. She left with questions no chart could answer.*

LINDA (fragile, halting): *It was just a cough. Seasonal, I thought. They ran tests. Said they needed to monitor me overnight. I remember the lights. The voices. Too many names. Too many pills.*

I asked what they were giving me. They said not to worry.

DJ: *Your doctor said that?*

LINDA: *He pointed to his nametag. Said that M.D. meant Make Decisions. Not Make Explanations.*

DJ: *And then?*

LINDA: *I woke up tied down. Purple wrists. No memory of how I got there. My daughter found me. She demanded the records. They were... incomplete.*

DJ (quiet): *And your body?*

LINDA: *They say all the meds given to me in such a short time have put me in complete organ failure and I only have a while left. My body remembers everything they forgot. Every pill. Every silence.*

[SFX: Distant echo of a heart monitor, then static]

CHAPTER 24 - RECORDS

Sarah returned to the precinct at City Hall to check the organ procurement records. Trinity General Hospital had more harvested organs than hospital s in four nearby states—cities much bigger than Rockford County. She circled the numbers in her notebook. It didn't add up.

She called a medical expert. "Is this normal?"

"No," they stated. "It's way too high. Something's wrong."

Sarah knew: this wasn't just about missing people. It was about profit.

Her phone buzzed. Unknown number.

She hesitated, then answered.

The voice on the other end was low, slurred—but urgent.

"The Lord giveth," the woman whispered. "Don't hang up."

Sarah froze. The voice wasn't familiar. Worn down. Like gravel soaked in gin.

"It's not just the ones who disappear," the woman said. "It's the ones who don't. The ones who make it out."

Sarah's pulse quickened. "Who is this?"

"Doesn't matter. You already know."

A pause. A breath. Then:

"They're giving antibiotics to people who don't need them. Not to treat anything. To keep the organs clean. Then they hit 'em with enough sedatives to drop a horse. Families get a call. 'Complications.' 'Cardiac arrest.' But they're not dead. Not yet."

Sarah's stomach turned.

"So, the hospital gets what it wants," she said. "This is murder."

The woman gave a bitter laugh.

"No, honey. Murder's clean. This is business."

Another pause. Then her voice dropped even lower.

"And if someone slips through? If they wake up, get discharged, make it home? Doesn't matter. The drugs keep working. The organs start to shut down. Liver, kidneys, heart. They die anyway. Just takes a little longer. Quiet. At home. No autopsy. The Lord taketh"

Sarah gripped the phone tighter.

"How do you know this?"

"Because I watched it happen. And I drank until I couldn't remember how many."

A rustle on the other end. A door creaked.

"the blood of the forgotten sanctifies the living."

"They're coming. Don't call back."

Quiet.

Sarah eyeballed the phone, the silence roaring in her ears.

She didn't know what was worse—the horror of what she'd just heard, or the fact that it confirmed everything she already feared.

She then began mapping the hospital like a crime scene—every timestamp, every intake code, every missing chart pinned to her hand-drawn floor plan. She wasn't just tracking people; she was tracking relationships. Routes. Gaps.

A moment of clarity came not from a confession or a clue, but from the walls themselves.

She was pretty sure the alibis were in the architecture.

Rooms mislabeled. Corridors rerouted. Logs that didn't match the physical layout. Trinity wasn't just hiding people—it was designed to. And once she recognized that, she stopped chasing witnesses and started chasing blueprints.

Records Department

She descended into the basement, where the air was thick with the scent of aged paper and floor wax. The lights buzzed overhead, casting long shadows across rows of filing cabinets and stacked boxes labeled in fading ink.

Willie Watson looked up from his desk, his reading glasses perched low on his nose. A retired facility manager turned records clerk, he had the faint fragrance of menthol and always had a story—about filing systems, about the old boiler room, about the time he helped Sarah buy her first car.

His eyes were tired, but kind.

"Well, if it isn't my favorite bloodhound," he said, voice gravelly. "What are we sniffing out today?"

Sarah dropped her folder on the counter. "Construction plans. Expansion layouts. Anything pre-renovation. Trinity General. City Hall. Underground waterways."

Willie raised an eyebrow. "Looking for ghosts?"

Sarah didn't smile. "Looking for the places they were buried."

He sighed, slid the sign-in sheet toward her. "That's a lot of paper kid! I'll need to pray extra Sunday, I fear. You always bring trouble with a smile."

"Only for people I like," she said, signing her name.

Two hours later, Sarah sat at the long wooden table, surrounded by rolled maps and diagrams with hints of mildew hanging in the air. She traced lines, compared layouts, marked inconsistencies.

The hospital's schematic was dated five years ago—three wings, a surgical annex, a basement level but, her photos showed doors that didn't exist on paper. Hallways that led nowhere. A service elevator that wasn't listed at all.

She walked over to Willie, who was now nursing a cup of tea and a menthol cough drop. "Are these all of them?"

He looked at her with a smirk and sighed.

"I know," she said softly. "But I wouldn't ask if it didn't matter."

He stood up slowly and unlocked a rusted cabinet. "These are the originals," he said, handing her a rolled set marked 1994. "Before Delaney started playing architect."

Sarah unrolled them carefully. The sub-levels were there—clearly marked: Service Corridors C1 through C4.

"But the public version ends at Corridor 2," she said.

In that same group was an old blueprint labeled *Trinity Expansion – 1998*. It showed a sealed corridor beneath the Harrow Wing.

She overlaid it with current maps and froze. The sealed corridor intersected directly with the Wells loading dock.

"Scrubbed in 2019," Willie said. "They called it streamlining. I call it hiding."

"Hidden how?"

He tapped his keyboard, then pointed at the screen. "They

reclassified the sublevels as 'non-essential infrastructure.' That flagged them for internal use only. No public access. No oversight."

"Off the books," Sarah muttered.

"Technically," he said. "Not illegal. Just buried deep enough to make you question your sanity."

She traced the erased lines. "Who signed off?"

"Delaney. The grandfather. No board review. No permits. Just a blue stamp that says 'Handled.'"

Sarah pulled the schematic for City Hall next. It was cleaner, but the underground waterways were a mess—twisting sublevels, outdated sewer lines, storm drains that led nowhere. Then she caught it, a maintenance conduit marked *inactive*, running directly beneath both City Hall and the hospital. Faded ink labeled it *Transfer Line 3A*. No access point listed. Just two initials: **SMH** and **Handled**.

Sarah circled it in red.

"They called it the Judge's Corridor," Willie said quietly. "Built it in '98. No permits. Just concrete and silence."

Sarah paused. "Why?"

"Legacy," he said. "Judge Delaney wanted a wing that couldn't be audited. Said it was for 'discretionary transfers.'"

Willie pulled up a file on the computer labeled *Infrastructure Expansion – Judicial Discretion*. He printed it off.

"This? You definitely never got from me."

Sarah walked to the printer and pulled the pages. Her eyes scanned maps, county recorder plot logs, tax assessments. On the plot map, she pointed to a shaded section.

"Wait… the courthouse and jail are located here?"

Willie nodded grimly.

Sarah leaned in. Her breath sharpened. "Are you telling me Judge Delaney owns all this land—and the county just leases it?"

Willie didn't speak. He just nodded.

Sarah blinked. "How is that even legal?"

Willie's voice was low. "The more people he puts in jail, the more the county kicks back to him. He's making millions off taxpayers. And probably making sure everyone gets sentenced."

Sarah's jaw tightened. "I've heard rumors—deputies getting bonuses, lawyers pushing plea deals. Trumped-up charges. Fast-track convictions."

Willie nodded again. "Henrietta Delaney's got a stake in the privately funded rehab centers too. So, if someone gets drug court or probation with mandatory treatment? They profit there too."

Sarah exhaled slowly. "They've monetized sentencing. Turned suffering into a business model."

Willie looked away. "They built a career on what they think a person's worth. And they never stop collecting. The good news is the Lord don't like ugly—and their reckoning day is coming."

Sarah gathered the maps, folded them carefully, and slid them into her bag.

Before she left, she turned to Willie. "You're not in this. I'll keep your name out of it."

He gave her a tired smile. "You never do but, thanks for pretending."

She kissed his cheek and walked out—her bag heavier, her pulse steady, her wit sharpened for whatever came next.

CHAPTER 25 – WIDOW X

Marcus walked down the gravel drive. The house was small, tucked behind a line of cedar trees, porch sagging slightly at the corners. Wind chimes clinked in the breeze—soft, metallic, like distant warnings.

She was already outside.

A woman in her early fifties. Gray streaks in her braid. Eyes that had stopped blinking for comfort years ago. She didn't look at him—she looked through him, like she was still searching for something she'd never find.

"You're Marcus Hayes," she said.

He nodded.

"Roy said you had something to share."

She didn't invite him in. Just gestured to the porch swing.

"I'll tell you here. I don't let people inside anymore. Not since they took him."

Marcus sat. She didn't.

"My husband was admitted last November. Just a backache, they said. He was a vet. PTSD, sure, but stable. Funny. Sharp. He built this porch with his own hands."

She paused, eyes scanning the tree line.

"Within days, they had him on nearly sixty medications. Heavy stuff. Antipsychotics. Antibiotics with clean cultures. They gave him a flu shot without asking. He started slurring. Said strange things. Told me to call Seal Team 7. Said they were going to kill him."

Marcus didn't interrupt.

"I tried to transfer him to the VA. They resisted. Said he'd die without CPAP and oxygen. Said his behavior was just PTSD but, I saw the chart. I printed it. I saw the drug they gave him—the one we told them he was allergic to. Sister med. Sent him into AFIB."

Her voice cracked, but she didn't stop.

"A friend who worked there saved him. Walked in, saw the chart, reversed it. Said he would've died that day. I got him out. He came home. Didn't need CPAP. Didn't need oxygen but, the damage was done. His organs were failing.

She finally sat beside Marcus, her hands trembling in her lap.

"Every new day was just a slower, crueler version of the one before. I could only stand there and watch the light dim—slowly, then all at once.

IT WAS QUIET, IT WAS RELENTLOUS!"

Marcus looked at her, unsure if he should speak.

"Did you report it?"

She let out a breath that wasn't quite a laugh.

"I wrote letters. Patient liaison. Administration. They said everything was medically necessary. Said he gave permission to people he didn't even know. Said he was competent—on the same day the chart said he wasn't."

She pulled a folder from beneath the swing. Thick. Warped from weather and grief.

"I have it all. Photos. Portal printouts. Whiteboard notes that don't match the records. Lies. He was dropped. Injured. They covered it up. Nurses wrote things that never happened. Called me names in his file."

Marcus took the folder gently.

"I'm filing a lawsuit," she said. "Sunday marks ninety days since I sent notice. Monday, I file. I don't care if they try to silence me. I've got a petition. A hundred signatures. A hundred stories. People who lost someone in that hospital and never got answers."

She looked out at the trees, her voice quieter now.

"When someone loses a parent, it's devastating but, this—this was the man I built a life with. Raised kids with. Became a grandparent beside. The one who knew my laugh, my fight, my quiet. The one who made me a 'we.'"

She turned to Marcus, eyes glassy but steady.

"He got the good card. He got to spend the rest of his life with me. Now I have the rest of my life to miss him."

Marcus swallowed hard.

"They'll come for you."

She nodded.

"Let them. I've already buried the worst they could take."

CHAPTER 26 – ALVEREZ

It was time to fill in the Captain and file her report. Time to make noise. Time to make sure Rockford County couldn't look away anymore.

Hart sat in the hallway outside Chief Alvarez's office; her folder balanced on her lap. Through the closed door, she could hear his voice—low, careful, threaded with tenderness.

"No, *mi amor*," he stated. "I'll be home by seven. I'll bring the soup. The one with ginger, like the doctor said."

A pause. Then softer: "I know. I miss you too."

Sarah looked down at her notes, trying not to listen. The tenderness in his voice was unmistakable—bone-deep, and startling in the context of the stale office.

"I'll call on my way," he asserted quietly. "You just rest. I've got this."

The line clicked. A moment passed. Then the door opened.

Alvarez stood in the frame, eyes tired but alert. He gestured her in.

"How's Mrs. Alverez?" Sarah says walking in "Maria is back home she is getting better" he gestures to a chair

The office was stale and unmoving. The walls were bare except for a faded flag and a photo of Alvarez shaking hands with the weasel, the Mayor. The blinds were drawn, casting gray stripes across the desk where he kept a picture of his wife. Sarah proceeded to lay her files open—names, dates, missing movement records, handwritten notes from families who hadn't stopped calling.

The Chief flipped through the pages slowly, his brow furrowed. He was a man built for caution—broad shoulders, clipped mustache, and a voice that rarely rose above neutral.

"These are serious claims," he said, eyebrows raised.

"They're true," Sarah replied, her voice steady. "People are disappearing from Trinity General. The facility's hiding it."

Alvarez leaned back, fingers steepled. "You have names, but no bodies. No official reports. No signed complaints."

Sarah leaned forward, her tone sharper. "That's the point. The reports are being erased to make sure you have nothing but names. The families are being ignored. The hospital is sorting people—who gets seen, who gets forgotten."

Alvarez sighed, the kind of sigh that came from years of political pressure and internal memos. "I need probable cause, not just suspicion." He glanced at the photo on the wall, then back at her. "You ever hear the story of the drunk under the streetlight?"

Sarah tilted her head.

"A policeman sees a drunk man searching for something under a streetlight. He asks what the drunk has lost. The man says his keys. They both look under the light. After a few minutes, the officer asks, 'Are you sure you lost them here?' The drunk replies, 'No, I lost them in the park.' 'Then why are you looking here?' And the drunk says, 'Because this is where the light is.'"

Sarah's eyes narrowed. "I get it, Chief. You're saying we're avoiding the darkness because the paperwork is easier under the fluorescent bulbs."

"I'm saying truth and wisdom—they're found where you least want to look."

Sarah nodded slowly. Then she leaned in, voice low and firm. "There's another story I prefer: Two little mice fell into a bucket of cream. The first mouse gave up and drowned. The second mouse wouldn't quit. He struggled so hard, he churned that cream into butter—and crawled out."

Alvarez gave a faint smile. "You're the second mouse."

SARAH: "And I'm not done churning. I'm just waiting for the butter to get hard enough to hit them with."

"I'll have the prosecutor look into it, but without more proof, it's hard to act. We need something concrete. A witness. A body. A paper trail that hasn't been shredded."

"If you wait for a body, you'll get one, but it'll be too late."

Sarah Hart gathered the folder, her voice clipped but steady. "You've got everything you need. If you sit on this, I'll assume you're part of it."

Alvarez didn't respond. He just watched her go, the silence in the room louder than any siren.

He stared at the desk—at the empty space where the folder had been. Then he reached into his drawer and pulled out a copy of the same intake log Sarah had shown him but, his version had a difference: a timestamp circled in red, and a signature that didn't match.

He studied it for a beat, then grabbed a sticky note from the corner of his desk and scribbled:

"Reynolds – timestamp mismatch. Vaughn's memo. Confirm chain SMH."

He set it beside the altered log, hand lingering.

The Captain just sat behind his desk, the blinds half-drawn, the air thick with old coffee and the weight of unfinished reports. A radio can be heard in the background *"This Saturday, join Trinity General Hospital and Starlight Baptist Church for our annual Racemakers for Pacemakers 5K! Whether you're walking, running, or cheering from the sidelines, every step helps support heart health and community care. Free screenings, live music, and a pancake breakfast for all participants. Trinity General—helping Buckles live longer, one beat at a time."*

A photo sat near the edge—his wife in a sunhat, smiling at the camera. Her eyes were bright, her skin pale.

Footsteps.

The knock was soft but deliberate.

He looked up.

Delaney stepped in first, blazer sharp, heels quiet on the tile. Grady followed, slightly tripping over his loose shoestring. He stood silent as ever, hands folded behind his back.

Homer lingered just outside the door, chewing gum and scrolling his phone—driver, muscle, witness. His thick fingers, usually smudged with dirt, carried a faint residue of bright blue paint beneath the nails, the exact shade of the hospital's logo.

Alvarez's eyes flicked to the sticky note.

He almost forgot.

Then, quick and quiet, he slid the papers into the drawer and pressed his palm over the note just as Delaney reached the chair.

She sat, crossed her legs, and smiled like a verdict.

"Ian, I assume you've reviewed the material?"

Alvarez nodded, fingers still covering the note.

"Good," she said. "Then let's talk about what's best—for

everyone."

Her eyes swept the room once, then landed on the photo. "She was stunning," she stated. "Still is, I'm sure. Though illness does tend to... harden the edges."

Alvarez didn't respond. His jaw tightened.

Delaney smiled like she hadn't said anything wrong. "I admire devotion, Chief. It's rare these days."

Grady moved to the corner, standing like a statue.

Alvarez: "You came for a reason."

Delaney placed a folder on his desk. "We're here to discuss discretion, and the cost of forgetting."

"What's this about?"

She opened the folder and turned it toward him. Inside were photos—grainy, timestamped. A man in uniform. A woman not his wife. A motel parking lot. Alvarez's jaw tightened.

"Where did you get these?"

Delaney said, "Let's not pretend I don't have reach."

He looked down at the photos again. "You're bluffing."

She slid another page across the table. A disciplinary report—typed, signed, but never filed. One that could be. It detailed "conduct unbecoming," "misuse of department resources," and "failure to disclose conflict of interest." Alvarez's throat tightened.

Then came the rest.

A stack of falsified donation receipts—each stamped with his department's foundation logo. They showed inflated amounts, backdated signatures, and line items that didn't exist, all traced back to Trinity General. "To a prosecutor, they looked like bribes".

"I'm offering you a choice," Delaney stated. "Not a threat."

Alvarez finally sat, voice low. "My wife is ill. She has a heart condition. She couldn't handle any of this. What do you want?"

Delaney leaned forward, voice calm, deliberate. "Discretion. When my facility is mentioned, you redirect. When my staff are questioned, you stall. When a detective starts asking too much, you remind her who funds your overtime."

Alvarez rubbed his temples. "You don't know what you're asking."

"I know exactly what I'm asking," Delaney said. "And I know what you almost recently lost and what you don't want to lose."

She stood, gathered the folder, and walked to the door. Grady opened it for her without a word. Homer waited just outside, arms crossed, watching the hallway.

Delaney paused, one hand on the doorframe.

"Oh, and Chief," she added, almost as an afterthought, "if you're still picking up that ginger soup—try the place on Sycamore. They use fresh turmeric. Better for inflammation."

Alvarez didn't move.

She smiled. "Just looking out for your wife." Shame, isn't it? Its always the pretty ones"

Then she was gone.

Alvarez stared at the empty doorway, the photo on his desk, and the folder still burning in his hands.

She knew. She'd been listening.

And now, she was watching.

CHAPTER 27 - "EXPOSE"

Earlier That Afternoon

Rebecca filed the divorce papers that morning. They hadn't been served yet, but the ink was dry. It felt like a formality—like she was already halfway gone.

She was sure Dr. Crawford was about to propose. He had that look lately. The lingering glances. The quiet invitations. The way he said *"My office is just upstairs"* like it meant something more.

He was smart. Handsome. Exciting. And even if he was just using her, she let herself believe it was more. Believing was easier than admitting she'd never felt worthy. Not since the Lunch Box. Not since she was *Little Orphan Fannie*, dancing for tips and pretending not to hear the jokes.

Low self-esteem wasn't a phase—it was a foundation. It didn't just shape her—it built her. Brick by brick. Tip by tip. It had shaped her walk, her voice, her choices. It had shaped Scott.

She met him the day his bride left him at the altar. He came into the club wrecked, raw. She danced for him. Stripped for him but, mostly, she listened. They fell in love in the quiet spaces—between songs, between drinks, between the grief he couldn't name and the hope she didn't trust.

Scott was safe. Solid. A good man. A great dad to their two little girls but, he was *Leave It to Beaver*, and she was ready for *Grey's*

Anatomy. She wanted clout. She wanted sparkle. She wanted to be the woman who walked into a gala with a doctor on her arm and didn't have to explain her past.

Crawford could give her that.

She'd convinced herself the divorce would be clean. That Scott would understand. That she could still co-parent, still care, still be kind but, she was done being the dependable one. She wanted to be chosen.

She was sure she was doing the right thing—at least she had been that morning when she left the papers on the counter. After a failed attempt to meet up with Crawford, Rebecca drove back home.

She stepped into Scott's office to grab her charger. He was in the shower, humming something soft and stupid. His laptop was open, screen still glowing.

She wasn't snooping. Not really. She was just... checking. Like any woman who's been underestimated too long.

But the filename caught her eye: Sarah – Trinity

This better not be that stupid ex of his—Sarah Hart, she thought.

She clicked.

The exposé unfolded in clean, surgical prose. Patient disappearances. Falsified records. A whistleblower buried in red tape. It was explosive. Award-worthy. And unmistakably Sarah's voice—tempered by Scott's edits.

Rebecca's jaw dropped.

Sarah had been talking to him. Late-night calls. Just work. She'd let it slide. She'd been rolling around in different sets of sheets with Crawford—and she had others—but Scott? Scott was hers.

Then she noticed: a Post-it stuck to the corner of the screen: CALL SARAH B4 PRINT — DANGER Red ink. Underlined twice.

Rebecca stared at it. Then peeled it off and crumpled it.

Just then, her phone buzzed. A text from Crawford.

She smiled, thumb hovering over the screen. *There you are, handsome.*

The message read:

I need space. This can't continue. The Lord's been convicting me— I've strayed too far. You're a good woman, Rebecca but, we both know you're not exactly First Lady material. The Lunch Box? Come on. That's not a past you can pray away.

No warmth. No apology. Just judgment wrapped in scripture and a slap of class cruelty.

The phrasing was careful but, the timing was not. He'd found out. Someone had told him. And now he was rewriting her into a cautionary tale.

Rebecca's smile vanished. Her throat tightened. She'd given him everything—access, silence, loyalty. She'd let herself believe she was becoming someone new. Someone worthy.

And now he was cutting her loose. Not just cutting—mocking.

Lunch Box? Come on. four words. One erasure.

She stared at the screen, the words burning into her. *Not First Lady material.*

And then she thought of **Eli Navarro**. The way he watched her —not like a fan, but like a threat. The way he said *"You've got presence"* like it was a compliment and a dismissal. The way he looked at the footage, at the timestamp, at the nurse who never blinked.

He thought she was just a face. She was about to prove him wrong.

No warmth. No apology. Just judgment wrapped in scripture and a slap of class cruelty.

Without any further thought, she looked back at the exposé on the laptop. It would hurt Crawford. Expose him. Shatter the pristine image he'd built.

It would be her revenge. Her resurrection. Her byline.

"If they're going to whisper about the Lunch Box, let them shout about this."

She clicked *Save As*, typed her name: By Rebecca Washman

Downloaded the file to the drive. Snapped the drive shut. Erased the file from the laptop.

"I want my girls to know I didn't just survive. I exposed the system that tried to bury me."

Walked to the bathroom door and hollered, "Love you! See you later."

Scott shouted something back—muffled by steam.

She was already gone.

CHAPTER 28 - SET MATCH

Emilee checked Room 312 just before lunch. Jordan Wells, 21, was recovering from ankle surgery after a soccer injury. He was sharp, funny, pre-med.

He was texting with one hand, I.V. in the other, earbuds in.

She paused at the door. "Still lobbying for pudding?"

Jordan (grinning): "I'm expanding my campaign. I want pudding *and* early discharge."

Emilee laughed. "You're stable, but not that stable."

Jordan glances at the hallway and his voice called out: "Dad! You bring me real food or just paperwork?"

Martin Wells stepped into the room, still in his work jacket, holding a folder and a coffee. "I brought you a contract dispute and a lukewarm latte. You're welcome."

Jordan groaned. "Worst care package ever."

Emilee smiled as she adjusted the IV. "He's been lobbying for pudding and early discharge. I told him he's not that charming."

Jordan (grinning): "I'm pre-med. I know how to fake stable vitals."

Martin: "He's been faking stable grades for years. You'll be fine, kid."

They laughed. Emilee felt the warmth ripple through the room. For a moment, it felt normal.

Just then, Sung, a CPN that worked as an admin stepped in—clipboard in hand, his badge swinging.

Sung: "Hey Jordan, quick signature needed. Just a standard form—hospital compliance."

Jordan: "What's it for? Is this the contract you were talking about dad /" they all laughed.

Sung (briskly): "I'm new here but I was told It's a D and NR, a digital routing form. 'Discharge and Notification Record.' We use it for post-op tracking."

Jordan: "You guys love acronyms."

Sung: "We live by them. Just sign at the bottom."

Jordan shrugged and signed.

Martin checked his watch. "I've got to go upstairs. Delaney's office. She sent me a new contract and forgot how math works."

Jordan gave him a mock salute. "Tell her I said hi. And that her I.V. tubing sucks."

Martin winked and headed to the administration floor.

Martin stood across from Delaney's desk, the contract folder open between them.

Martin: "These numbers aren't what we discussed. I sent in a proposal—double last year's rate. Just to cover manpower and fuel."

Delaney (coolly): "We didn't discuss anything. You submitted a proposal. This is our counter."

Martin Wells stood stiffly across from Delaney's desk.

Martin: "These numbers don't make sense. You're ordering double the tubing and half the filters. And the billing—who's approving this?"

Delaney (coolly): "We're streamlining. If you want to stay on contract, you'll comply."

Martin: "You rewrote the vendor agreement. I'm getting paid half of what I used to."

Delaney (leaning in): "If you want to keep your mouth shut and your business intact, I suggest you stop asking questions."

Martin: "It's not a counter. It's robbery. Wells Supply has been your sole supplier for twenty years. My father got this bid decades ago. I haven't raised rates once since I took over."

Delaney: "Then you should be grateful. Loyalty is a currency. You're still cashing it."

Martin: "Not anymore. I'm not renewing.

Delaney: "Push this? You have a contract until next year and it renews at my discretion, not yours! Your father understood that why is it so hard for you to?"

Martin: "I'm cancelling our contract with you, If I need to go to court over it then I will you can't control me or my business. We keep your secrets but if you push this, there may be legal consequences."

Delaney leaned back, her smile thin.

Delaney: "Is that a threat?"

Martin: "Yes. You can consider it a threat."

She tapped the folder once, then closed it.

Delaney: "Well then. Set, match."

Martin's jaw clenched. He turned and walked out, muttering under his breath.

Two hours later, the overhead speaker crackled. "Code Blue – Room 312."

Emilee ran.

Inside: chaos. Alarms screaming. Jordan's face pale, lips blue.

Martin was standing in the room, frozen in the corner, eyes wide.

Emilee reached for the crash cart, but the attending waved her off. "**DNR**," he said. "We're calling it."

Emilee froze. "What?"

He pointed to the chart. "Signed this morning."

Martin screams "what?" calling it? Why are you saving him? hands shaking.

Doctor: "I'm so sorry. We did everything we could."

Martin's knees buckled. He fell to the ground

Delaney walked past 312 without slowing. Her heels clicked once, twice, then faded.

Crawford walked in and put his hand on Martins shoulder and started to pray. He was looking up just as Delaney passed.

His eyes met hers.

A confused look, almost shock.

Then realization.

After the room cleared, Emilee pulled Jordan's file. **DNR** signed

No proxy. No family. Just a scribbled initial. Stamped in blue: **HANDLED**. It wasn't a **Discharge and Notification Record** it was a **Do Not Resuscitate** – He didn't read the fine print and that assistant lied to him and now he's gone!

Her stomach turned. She'd spoken to him less than an hour ago. He was laughing. Awake. Planning discharge.

Now he was gone. And his father the man whose company was the biggest vendor of hospital supplies to Trinity General

Hospital had watched it happen.

CHAPTER 29 – GOING LIVE

Inside, **Rebecca Washman** stepped into the Channel 3 studio with purpose, heels clicking like a countdown.

She didn't pause. Didn't smile. Didn't blink.

She breezed past the interns. Past the segment producer. Past the weather guy rehearsing his lines.

And past **Eli Navarro**, who looked up from his notes just in time to catch her eye.

She didn't say a word. Just gave him a look—cool, cutting, electric. *Watch this, amateur.*

Then she was gone.

A drive was tucked in her bra. Her blazer was sharp. Her smile was ready.

She found **Ed** in the control room, mid-conversation with legal.

"I've got something urgent," she said, handing him the drive. "Exclusive. We need to go live."

Ed took it, confused. "What is this?"

"Just watch."

He plugged it in. Scanned the file. His eyes widened.

"Lord almighty," he muttered. "This is huge. Where did you—"

"I've been working it for weeks," she lied, smooth as glass.

Ed nodded, already waving the tech team over. "Bless your heart. We'll get you on at six. This is going to blow up."

Rebecca smiled—radiant and venomous.

"Six?" she said.

Ed looked up. "We need time to vet it. Legal's gotta clear it. We'll tease it at five, drop it at six."

"No," she said. "We're not teasing. We're not waiting."

"Rebecca—"

"I'm going live," she said. "Now."

Ed blinked. "That's not how we do things."

"It is today."

She turned toward the studio floor, already moving. The techs looked up, startled. The floor director stepped in, headset half-on.

"Rebecca—what's happening?"

She didn't answer. She was already in position.

She thought "They think I'm just a face. This story proves I'm the spine."

Ed stood frozen, the drive still in his hand. Legal hadn't seen it. The newsroom hadn't cleared it but, the anchor chair was hers. And she was about to earn it.

Across town, Scott Washman sat at his desk at the *Sentinel*, searching for the drive with the final draft of the exposé he'd finished at home earlier. The headline was tight. The facts were solid. Sarah had risked everything to get this far, and he'd promised to protect her story.

He checked the shared drive. Nothing. His stomach turned.

In the background he hears the television "Breaking News from Channel 3's Rebecca Washman"

There she was; On one of the overhead monitors, his wife, Rebecca Washman—anchor of the 6 o'clock news, queen of the teleprompter—was already seated at the desk, mic hot, camera rolling. Her jewel-toned blazer caught the light. Her smoky voice hadn't spoken yet, but her smile was already loaded.

She looked into the camera, eyes sharp, voice steady.

"This is Rebecca Washman, and tonight we bring you a story that will change everything you thought you knew about healthcare in Rockford County…"

LIVE.

"In breaking news tonight," she continued, her tone stripped of its usual hospital platitudes, "Trinity General Hospital is under scrutiny after anonymous allegations surfaced regarding patient mismanagement and missing people. Hospital officials deny wrongdoing, calling the claims 'unfounded and inflammatory.'"

The video techs scrambled for footage. They found it. The footage was slick—B-roll of the Hospital's pristine lobby, a soundbite from Dr. Crawford looking calm and concerned, and a closing line from Rebecca:

"We'll continue to follow this developing story. For now, officials urge the public not to jump to conclusions."

Scott froze.

She was live. With his story.

He knew that look. He'd written the pieces that got her there —crafted the narratives, shaped the tone, built the trust. He'd stepped back when the station said couples couldn't share the spotlight. Took the quieter job. Let her rise.

It was noble. It was love.

But this exposé wasn't for her, it wasn't hers! It was Sarah's, and Rebecca had stolen it.

Scott felt a lump in his throat.

She had no right.

He glared at the screen, the words rolling out of her mouth like velvet-wrapped theft.

He didn't feel noble anymore.

He didn't feel married.

He stared at her face—poised, polished, perfect. For the first time, she was ugly to him.

He grabbed his phone, dialing Sarah's number. No answer.

He turned the TV off.

CHAPTER 30 – "THE PRETTY ONES"

Sarah pushed through the double doors of the station, her pulse still spiking from what she just saw. She needed answers—now. Why had he let his wife hijack the story? What was he hiding?

But the sidewalk wasn't clear.

A massive parade float loomed across the entrance to the lot, parked at an angle like it had been abandoned mid-route. It was gaudy and overbuilt—papier-mâché angels, gold fringe, and a banner that read *"Buckles Gospel Jubilee – Faith in Motion!"* The undercarriage hissed with heat, and a speaker crackled with static gospel music, like heaven had a bad connection.

Sarah stopped short. "Oh good," she muttered. "A holy traffic jam."

She tried to cut around it, but the float blocked both walkways. She had to step off the curb, weaving between folding chairs, half-eaten funnel cakes, and a tangle of extension cords that looked one spark away from divine intervention.

A volunteer in a neon vest waved at her distractedly. "Sorry, ma'am—float's stuck. Generator overheated."

Sarah ducked under a sagging streamer. "Of course it did. Nothing says 'Faith in Motion' like a flaming engine and a detour through snack debris."

She stepped over a tipped cooler and nearly tripped on a rogue tambourine. "If I get electrocuted by a gospel float, I swear I'm haunting this town."

The volunteer blinked, unsure whether to laugh or call someone.

Sarah didn't wait. She was already moving—heels scraping pavement, adrenaline rising, and sarcasm trailing behind her like confetti.

By the time she reached the lot, she was sweating, irritated, and half-distracted by the text she was composing in her head. She didn't notice the silence. Didn't notice the way the air felt heavier near her car.

She unlocked the door and tossed her bag onto the passenger seat.

That's when the heavy air of sweat, Bleach ,and something metallic curled around her like a threat.

She froze.

But she didn't hear the soft shift of weight behind her.

A hand clamped over her mouth—fast, deliberate, no panic in the grip. Just control.

She thrashed, elbow jerking backward, but the arm was already braced. Strong. Trained.

Then the sting.

Cold metal against her neck. A syringe. The needle slid in clean.

Her breath hitched.

A man's voice, low and close: **"It's always the pretty ones."**

Her legs went first—tingling, then numb. The sensation crawled upward, ice burning through her veins. Her fingers twitched against the steering wheel, trying to fight, trying to reach the horn, but her body was slipping.

Her vision blurred. The dashboard lights smeared into halos.

Her chest felt heavy, like gravity had doubled.

She tried to scream. Nothing came.

The voice leaned in again, breath warm against her ear. **"Stop digging. Or next time, it's permanent."**

Then silence.

Just the soft click of the door unlocking from the inside.

CHAPTER 31- THE DRAWING

Emilee moved through her shift like normal, but her eyes were sharp. Watching everything.

Near the east wing, she spotted a new security guard—someone she hadn't seen before—speaking with Spencer. They both stopped talking as she passed, tracking her every movement in silence.

She kept her head down and made her way to the supply closet. Inside, she started pulling "Wells Supply" boxes toward her, checking each one. She didn't know what she was looking for—just that something might be hidden.

Then she saw it. A pile of folders tucked behind the paper towel boxes. She grabbed them, flipping through quickly.

Each one tied to a patient with a questionable chart: Sepsis with clean labs. Unexplained transfers. Sudden DNR overrides.

Her chest tightened. This was getting to be too much. Was it even worth it?

She tossed the folders into the trash. One paper fluttered out and landed face-up on the floor.

A drawing. A dog with a short ear. Childlike. Uneven. She wasn't sure why, but she crouched, snapped a photo, and sent it to Sarah.

Then she saw it—blue ink, faint in the corner: **SMH.** She zoomed in. Circled it in her notebook.

She pulled the folders back out of the trash. Next one—same stamp. And the next.

SMH. She'd heard it before. "Standard Medical Hold." "SMH flagged—no psych consult needed." "Subjective Mental Health," someone had said once. Used when symptoms were reported but not verified.

She'd always assumed it was intake shorthand. Bureaucratic noise. But now, with the stickers, the riddles, the Harrow Wing studio still fresh in her mind— It felt heavier. Intentional.

She circled the stamp again. Added it to her anomaly list. She didn't know what it meant, but it kept showing up—always on the files that felt wrong.

Then a strange thought hit her. **Sarah Hart.** Could her middle name be **Marie**?

Just then, a man in a suit walked in. No badge. No clipboard. He started loading supply boxes onto a cart like he belonged there.

He looked up, met her eyes, and smiled. It didn't reach his eyes.

"Can I help you?" she asked.

"Just transferring some supplies to the E.R.," he said smoothly.

Emilee nodded and walked out, but her hands were shaking. She knew what this meant. They were cleaning up.

She rushed back to the trash, spotted two more folders she'd missed, and wrapped them in her sweater.

She glanced at the clock. Her shift was over.

Locker. Bag. Badge. She slipped into the staff-only stairwell, cutting through two wings she knew better than most. Her knowledge of the building had become a survival skill.

Halfway down the second flight, her shoe caught on a loose tread. She stumbled, caught herself, and looked down.

A thin plastic card lay wedged between the steps and the wall—half-covered in dust.

She bent down, pried it loose.

Access: Sub-Level 2 – Expired The barcode was faded. The name field was blank.

Her breath hitched.

She tucked it into her pocket and kept moving, but her pace slowed. That stairwell didn't connect to Sub-Level 2. Not officially.

She exited through an unmarked door on the first floor and headed toward the front. The halls were hushed, but not calm. Too many closed doors. Too many glances that didn't linger.

At the front desk, a man in a gray suit stood waiting. Clipboard. Thick envelope. He didn't look up.

Emilee slowed, heart pounding.

"Emilee Vaughn?" he asked.

She nodded, instinctively straightening her badge.

He handed her the envelope. **"You've been served."**

She blinked. **"Served?"**

"Civil summons. Rockford County. Case number's on the front."

He turned and walked out without another word.

Emilee stared at the envelope. Her name was printed in bold.

Below it: **Rockford County Medical Review Board v Vaughn**

She tore it open with shaking hands.

Inside: A notice of hearing. A complaint alleging breach of duty. A reference to a patient she'd never treated. A signature from a judge she didn't recognize.

The paperwork claimed she'd falsified a discharge summary. The date matched the day Tommy Reynolds's documentation was altered.

She inhaled fury.

She flipped to the last page.

Stamped in blue: **SMH.**

Not a warning. Not a reprimand. A declaration of war.

CHAPTER–32 FM DIAL

Sarah blinked hard, her head pounding. The car seat pressed against her spine like concrete. Her mouth was dry. Her limbs felt heavy, slow—like she'd been poured into herself wrong.

She tried to sit up. The world tilted.

She couldn't drive. Couldn't focus. Could barely see through the fog behind her eyes.

So, she turned on the radio.

Static. Then a voice—bright, polished, merciless.

"…and in breaking news, Channel 3 confirms that Trinity General Hospital is under investigation following a leaked exposé published by Rebecca Washman…"

Sarah froze.

"…The report includes firsthand interviews, internal hospital documents, and a timeline of alleged misconduct. Sources remain anonymous, but the voice in the leaked audio appears to match a local law enforcement official…"

Her stomach dropped.

She knew that voice. It was hers.

She whispered, "He gave her my exposé."

The radio kept going, cheerful and damning.

"…Community leaders have called for a Town Hall meeting tonight at 7PM to address the allegations…"

Sarah slumped back in the seat, pulse rising, breath shallow.

Scottie hadn't called. No warning. No heads-up. Just silence—and now this.

She stared at the dashboard, eyes unfocused. "His wife," she muttered. "The one who cheats like it's cardio. The one who told me she wished I were dead."

The betrayal wasn't just professional. It was intimate. Surgical. He hadn't just leaked her investigation. He'd handed it to someone who wanted her erased.

The radio crackled again.

"…The report has already sparked online outrage, with thousands sharing the story under the hashtag #TrinityTruth…"

Sarah closed her eyes. The storm had broken. And she was still in the wreckage

CHAPTER 33 – THE FUNNEL

Marcus sat at Roy's desk, the vinyl chair creaking beneath him. A flash runs through his mind.

KANDAHAR OUTSKIRTS, NIGHT OPS - The desert wind howled. Moonlight flickered across jagged rock. Hayes crouched low behind a collapsed wall, fingers smeared with grease and sand. His left leg throbbed—shrapnel.

He pulled a multitool, rerouting a cracked radio with stripped wire. "Call it in," Marcus stated. "Then get ready to move."

He grabbed a flare, cracked it, and shoved it into a busted fuel line. "That's gonna blow," Roy muttered.

"Not yet," Marcus replied. "It'll smoke first. Make 'em think we're burning."

They moved fast—Marcus limping, Roy covering. They emerged behind the ridge. Roy took point. Three shots. One grenade. Clean. Surgical.

"You pulled the trigger," Hayes stated later. "I just built the door."

Back in the present, the coffee Roy handed him smelled like burnt rubber, but Marcus took a sip anyway. The shelter was quiet—too quiet for midmorning.

Roy leaned against the filing cabinet, arms crossed, watching the TV in the corner. There it was. "**Ghost** Admissions: Veterans Vanish at Trinity General Hospital ," Rebecca Washman reporting. The headline stretched across the bottom of the screen like a wound.

Marcus set the coffee down and turned to Roy. "Sarge, you ever hear of anyone not coming back from a checkup?" he asked, voice low.

"Gunny, you know as well as I do, people disappear all the time," Roy said finally. "Especially vets."

Marcus leaned forward. "You ever take someone to Trinity and not see them again?"

Roy looked away. "I drive a lot of guys. I don't keep tabs."

Marcus's eyes narrowed. "You keep records. You sign the transport sheets. Sarge, you know who goes in."

Roy's jaw tightened. "You think I know? Or you think there was a choice?"

Hayes stared at him, it all began to click, his voice cracking. "How does a guy like you get turned? How'd they compromise a sergeant like you? You're the guy who pulled three men out of a burning Humvee! You're the guy who stood up to command about that friendly fire report! How could you become this?"

Roy just sat down slowly, like the weight had finally caught up. "We may not be in uniform," he stated, "but this is a war, Gunny. We're all smack dab in the middle of it."

"Why?" Marcus demanded, the word sharp with pain.

"They tested me," Roy muttered. "Random urine test, I was dirty. Delaney made it disappear. Said I could keep the job, the car, the housing. Said I just had to help her keep things smooth."

Marcus's voice was ice. "Smooth? You betrayed them for a paycheck?"

"She said the vets trust me. That I could help them help so many more people. That I could make it easy for the greater good."

Marcus stared at him. "You're the funnel."

"I didn't know what they were doing at first," Roy stated. "I thought it was just bad paperwork. Then one of the guys—Darnell—he didn't come back. I asked. They said he transferred, but no one ever saw him again."

Marcus leaned forward, elbow on his knee. "What about Natalie? You knew her. She trusted you. You sure you don't know more than you let on?"

Roy didn't answer right away. "I knew she was sharp," he said finally. "Didn't talk much, but she watched everything. Like she was building a case in her head."

Marcus waited.

"But I didn't know what she was into," Roy swore. "I swear. She asked questions, yeah. Took notes, but nobody told me anything. I just drove."

Marcus studied him. "You didn't wonder why she disappeared?"

"I did," Roy admitted. "But wondering doesn't get you answers around here. It gets you replaced or disappeared." Roy's head dropped and looked down.

Marcus didn't speak, but he believed him. For now.

Marcus looked at the TV. The screen flickered between faces and timestamps. "You're going to help me fix this," he stated.

Roy didn't answer, but he didn't say no.

CHAPTER 34 - AND A – 1

Rebecca sat in her dressing room, wiping off her makeup with slow, deliberate strokes. Her phone buzzed. Crawford.

She smiled, then answered. **"You saw the segment?"** she asked, a smug lilt in her voice.

"I did," he said flatly. **"You shouldn't have run it."**

"I thought you'd be grateful."

"I told you I needed time."

Rebecca's smile faded, leaving a cold feeling on her mouth. **"You said you needed space. That's different."**

There was a pause. Heavy. Deliberate.

"I don't need a little orphan Fannie in my world," Crawford said with disgust.

Rebecca didn't flinch. She blinked once, then leaned forward, voice low and surgical.

"You mean the girl who got dragged through the system, lied to by doctors, and left bleeding in a hallway while men in suits debated her billing code?" **"You mean the girl who survived?"**

Silence.

"You don't want Fannie in your world?" she continued. **"Then maybe you shouldn't have built one that needs her to**

disappear."

Crawford exhaled. **"I'm going to be seeing someone else. It's not personal. It's just… cleaner."**

Rebecca laughed bitterly, the sound brittle and fake. **"Emilee Vaughn? She's not even your type. She's plain. Quiet. You'll get bored."**

Crawford's voice was calm, final. **"I'm done, Rebecca."**

Then, before hanging up, he added softly: **"Let all things be done decently and in order."** *1 Corinthians 14:40*

The line clicked dead.

Rebecca stared at her reflection—perfect hair, perfect teeth, perfect Story. Surely a huge breaking story like this deserved a Murrow….

The city outside the news studio window was a bruise-purple blur under the first heavy drops of rain. She walked back into the studio, the **ghost** of her own voice still buzzing in the air from the explosive broadcast that had just skewered the city's largest hospital .

Her phone vibrated. Unknown Number. She frowned and swiped to answer. "Hello?"

The voice on the other end was quiet, feminine, and devoid of inflection—like an automated recording struggling to sound human. "A brilliant broadcast, Ms. Washman. Truly. A shame to burn a promising career so quickly. Such a messy, predictable tragedy when things aren't **handled** *discreetly*."

A cold knot tightened in Rebecca's stomach she felt like she knew the voice. "Who is this?"

A soft, almost pitying sigh. "Just a friend, Rebecca. Concerned about your health. A good journalist knows that sometimes, the biggest stories are the ones you leave *unwritten*. Sleep well."

The line went dead. The silence that followed was louder than the dial tone. This wasn't some angry viewer; this was calculated. The hair stood up on the back of her neck.

She rushed down to the deserted lobby, the strange, cold dread making her hands shake. She had burned bridges all day—the hospital, her marriage, her dignity. Now, someone was sending a message.

She frantically dialed the one person she desperately needed to hear from. Scott.

The call went straight to voicemail.

Beep. "Scott, it's me. I... I know you're probably ignoring my calls, and you have every right to. I've been such an idiot. A complete, self-absorbed fool. Dr. Crawford—he ended it, just a few hours ago. He didn't want the mess, the scandal, any of it. He's a coward, and I see it now. I see everything now."

She pushed through the revolving doors and into the spitting rain. Her heels clicked urgently on the concrete as she ran toward the employee parking garage.

"I filed those Divorce papers because I was lost. I was looking for excitement, but all I ever had was the real thing with you. Scott, I'm so sorry. I love you. I love you, and I need you to call me back. Please. Let's talk. Let's fix this. I'm heading home now. Please, call me."

She ended the message, clutching the phone to her chest. It was a plea, a confession, a prayer—a message too late for a man she had pushed away.

She pulled out onto the main street. The rain was an instant monsoon, the wipers fighting a losing battle against the deluge. She gripped the wheel, eyes straining, her mind still replaying the icy voice on the phone and Scott's silence.

Suddenly, a blur of blue burst through the downpour, appearing to drift sideways. It was a large van. There was no time to swerve, no time to scream.

The sound was a sickening, tearing screech of metal and glass, followed by a thick, heavy *thud*. Her little convertible rolled end over end, the world dissolving into flashes of violent light and shadow.

Rebecca woke and *was hit by the stench* of gasoline and wet asphalt. Pain bloomed in her shoulder and ribs. She was lying on the ground, the drizzle hitting her face. A deep, agonizing groan escaped her lips. She was alive.

A few feet away, her car was a twisted, unrecognizable ruin. The blue van was idling, dark and massive, perpendicular to her wreckage.

She pushed herself up onto her elbow. Her world tilted; the streetlights spun into sickly yellow halos. Dizzy, but moving.

Her phone lay face-down in a puddle nearby. She reached for it, her fingers scraping the rough ground, desperate to call Scott back. To hear his voice one last time.

Then, two large shapes moved into her field of vision.

She saw them first: two pairs of men's black work boots, thick-soled and heavy, one of the boots was untied, planted firmly on the wet pavement directly in front of her face.

She looked up, squinting through the stinging rain. Two hulking figures stood over her. They were nondescript, wrapped in dark, heavy rain gear—unreadable.

"**Help**," she rasped, her voice barely audible. "**Please… call 911. I'm hurt.**"

The taller man bent down, his shadow swallowing her. His face was a blank void beneath the hood—no expression, no hesitation.

He crouched beside her. Then, in a slow, deliberate gesture, he spit on her. The stench hit first—metallic, chemical, laced with spray paint. He smeared her lipstick with his finger, dragging it from her mouth to her cheek like a signature.

She tried to scream. Nothing came. Her limbs flailed, weak and disjointed. She spun in the wet gravel, unable to stand, unable to flee. She just needed to run.

He let her squirm. Watched her struggle. Then grabbed her arm with blue-stained fingers—tight, unyielding.

She froze. Paralyzed by the certainty of what was coming. Right here. Middle of the road. In the rain.

The second man adjusted his glove, his boot untied, his voice sing-song and casual.

"Hold her?"

The first man climbed on top of her, straddling her chest. Heavy. Suffocating. His knees pressed against her ears. Her arms pinned. Only her head could move—barely.

He gripped her hair, forcing her gaze upward. Rain poured into her eyes. She blinked, desperate to see his face.

The first one leaned in, voice lilting like a twisted lullaby.

"It's always the pretty ones." "And a one… and a two…"

His boot lifted. Then dropped.

A white-hot burst of pain. A crunch that echoed through her skull.

Again. And again. Each stomp more violent than the last.

The second man finally stepped back, motioning to stop. Rebecca's body was limp. The only sound was the rain—and her faint, gurgling cries.

The spray-paint man raised his foot. Paused. Then nudged her shoulder.

No movement.

The other man bent down, tied his shoe, and pulled out a phone tone completely calm and neutral. "Hello? we just seen a very terrible car crash on Elm Street. Head-on. Looks like the pretty lady is hurt bad."

They waited until they heard the distant wail of sirens, then slowly, deliberately, they walked away leaving the van with no license plates behind and walked off calmly into the curtain of rain.

CHAPTER 35 – HEADACHE

Across town, Sarah was just waking up in her car, head pounding from the sedative, when her phone buzzed.

Scott's name lit up the screen.

She answered groggily, voice raw.

"Did you leak it?"

"No," Scott replied. "I swear. I didn't even know it aired until I saw it live. It wasn't from the paper. It was the station—Rebecca."

Sarah's blood ran cold.

"She knew," she whispered. "She knew it would put me in danger."

Scott was silent for a beat.

"Why would she do that?"

Sarah didn't answer.

But she knew.

"Listen I'm not even calling about that, Rebecca was in a horrible accident she is at Trinity now I am on my way there but it just seems like more to the story – can you meet me there?"

"More to the story what do you mean?" she started then said "I … of course … I'm on my way".

She hung up and stirred in the driver's seat, head throbbing, mouth dry. Her neck stung where the needle had gone in. Her limbs felt heavy, like she'd slept in wet clothes. Her feet felt like wet sandbags. The car's interior spun slowly. The sedative hadn't worn off—it had just retreated.

Another buzz.

A message from Emilee.

No text. Just an attachment.

Sarah opened it.

A drawing.

She admired the crooked ear, the soft eyes. The lines were uneven but familiar—drawn with care, not skill. She exhaled a sob she didn't know she'd been holding.

Tommy used to draw all the time. On napkins, receipts, the backs of flyers. He'd sketch his family dog—Bishop—with one ear shorter than the other, always curled at the tip like it was listening sideways.

Bishop had been his anchor during the worst of it. After the deployments. After the breakdowns. That dog had slept beside him through every panic spiral, every night terror.

Sarah remembered one drawing in particular—Tommy had handed it to her after a group session.

"He's not much," he'd said, "but he never leaves."

This looked like that.

She ran her thumb gently along the edge of the phone, as if it might speak. The pencil was smudged. The ear was still crooked.

This wasn't just a sketch.

It was a message.

It was motivation.

She gripped the steering wheel, knuckles white. Every movement was a negotiation, but she had to move.

Had to get back to Trinity General Hospital not for Rebecca but for Scott…

She forced the vehicle into motion. *Every light is double. The steering wheel—grease.* They took the fight out of her muscles, but not her lungs. *Pull over, I'm dead. Crash, I'm dead—and they win.* Keep driving.

She blinked against the light.

The Hospital parking lot was quiet; the sky still bruised from the storm. Her phone buzzed with missed calls. She didn't remember driving here. She didn't remember leaving the station. The radio was on. The story was everywhere. D.J. says: "Trinity General Under Investigation: Missing Patients, Altered Records, Organ Protocols Questioned." "Federal Oversight Team Arrives in Rockford County." "Whistleblower Claims Hospital Used Diagnosis Codes to Disappear Vulnerable Patients."

Then she remembered, Scott, Rebecca… she slowly emerged from her car – parked sideways in an overflow lot. She couldn't yet run but at least now she could walk sorta straight.

CHAPTER 36 - THE BODY IN 3A

The rain hadn't let up. It pounded the ER roof in waves, a relentless percussion that matched the chaos inside.

Rebecca Washman arrived at Trinity General on a stretcher, barely breathing. Her face was a ruin of blood and bone; her limbs twisted unnaturally beneath soaked blankets. The paramedics shouted vitals as they wheeled her through the automatic doors, but even they looked shaken.

Scott was already there when Sarah arrived, pale and trembling, her own body still reeling from the sedatives she'd been pumped with hours earlier. She found him in the ICU waiting area, hunched forward in a plastic chair, hands clasped between his knees like he was trying to hold himself together.

"She's in 3A," he said without looking up. "Four different doctors came in. I don't know what the hell they're saying. I don't understand any of it."

Sarah followed his gaze through the glass. Rebecca was unrecognizable. Her face was swollen beyond imagination; her nose flattened into the plane of her cheeks. A cervical collar braced her neck. Her arms were wrapped in gauze and rigid splints. Tubes snaked from her mouth, her arms, her chest.

Scott's eyes were red and raw. He looked like he hadn't blinked in hours.

"I'll find someone," Sarah said softly. "We'll get answers."

She found Emilee near the nurses' station; a paramedic was walking away from her.

"Can you find someone who can explain what's going on with Rebecca in 3A?" Sarah asked.

Emilee nodded. "I'll look at the chart. Compare it with what that Paramedic just told me and see what I can figure out."

Minutes later, Sarah returned to 3A with two coffees. She handed one to Scott, who took it with shaking hands but didn't drink.

Emilee entered with Dr. Crawford.

Scott looked up. His eyes narrowed. Then, without a word, he threw the coffee down and lunged.

"YOU—!"

His fist connected with Crawford's nose in a sickening crunch. Blood spattered across the doctor's collar. Sarah and Emilee grabbed Scott, pulling him back as he collapsed to the floor, sobbing.

Crawford straightened slowly, dabbing at his nose with a handkerchief. He gave them a look—stoic, almost amused – this obviously was not the first time this happened to him. Then he closed his eyes.

"Let us pray," he said.

The room froze.

He launched into a prayer—measured, profound, disturbingly appropriate. He spoke of suffering, of surrender, of the body as a vessel and the soul as a flame. When he finished, even Sarah found herself blinking back tears.

"I understand your anger," he said to Scott, his voice warm now, almost fatherly. "You've suffered a terrible blow. I want to help you understand what's happening."

He walked to the whiteboard, flipped on the backlight, and clipped up a series of X-rays.

"This," he said, pointing, "is her femur. Shattered in two places. Here, and here."

He moved to the next slide.

"Her C1 vertebra—completely fractured. The impact snapped her neck back, severing the spinal cord. She's paralyzed from the neck down."

He paused. "Her face… the trauma was extensive. Multiple fractures to the zygomatic arches, orbital floors, nasal bridge. The swelling is obscuring most of her features."

Sarah stared at Rebecca's face. It didn't look human. The nose was gone—just a swollen, flattened mass. Her eyes were sealed shut, the lids purple and ballooned. Her lips were split, her jaw slack.

How could this happen in a car crash? Sarah thought. I've seen wrecks. I've seen ejections. I've never seen this.

Emilee stepped closer to the X-rays. Her eyes narrowed. Thinking back to what the paramedic just told her moments before. He said "I've been to hundreds of car accidents in my career; I have never seen a crash victim with these kinds of injuries. What I have seen is domestic assault victims with these injuries".

"Dr. Crawford," she said, "can you go back to the cranial scan?"

He turned the light back on.

Emilee who has unfortunately seen her fair share of car accidents and horrible domestic assault cases pointed. "This—this isn't consistent with a steering wheel impact."

Crawford turned, brow raised.

"See here?" she said to Sarah. "The cheekbones are shattered inward. Not from a single blow—but multiple. And the orbital rims—both sides. That's not typical of a frontal collision."

Sarah leaned in. "And the forehead fracture…"

"Exactly," Emilee said. "It's linear, but shallow. Like a boot tread. And the occipital flattening—look at the back of the skull. That's not from hitting a headrest. That's from being driven into pavement. Repeatedly."

Crawford's voice cut in, smooth and unbothered. "High-speed trauma can present in unusual ways. The body is unpredictable under stress."

He smiled, blood still drying beneath his nose.

"If you need anything," he said, "have the nurses call me."

He turned and walked out.

Scott sat in silence, staring at the floor. His hands trembled in his lap.

"Not my Rebecca," he whispered. "Not her. Not my girls. Her parents…"

"Sarah," Emilee said, voice low. "Come here." her voice tightened. She'd seen this before—an actress dragged behind a car; a teenager left in a ditch. The motive was always the same: break the face first. She pointed at the X-ray again. "This isn't just trauma. I started as a nurse in Los Angeles California, I have seen it all and, in my opinion, this looks targeted

Emilee's voice dropped to a whisper. "This wasn't an accident. It was a message."

Sarah stared at the scan, her jaw clenched. "Controlled," she said. "Like someone needed to break her

Emilee whispers "without killing her"

Sarah whispered back "—yet."

Scott didn't move..

Emilee stepped back, eyes scanning the hallway. "We need to get a copy of this chart. Before it's altered."

Sarah nodded. "I'll talk to the paramedic again. See if he's willing to go on record."

Emilee hesitated. "If he does, he'll be targeted. They don't just erase patients here. They erase witnesses."

Sarah looked at Rebecca through the glass. Her body was still. Her face—what was left of it—was a map of violence.

"She's not the first," Sarah said. "But she's going to be the last."

CHAPTER 37 - THE HONOR WALK

The ICU room was still humming when Dr. Crawford left. He'd explained the scans, the fractures, the prognosis. Scott hadn't said a word. Sarah and Emilee lingered behind, staring at the lightboard.

Outside, a night parade was crossing the hospital entrance—marching bands, baton twirlers, floats decked in red, white, and blue. Music drifted in through the sealed windows, muffled but unmistakable. Children were clapping and waved flags. Confetti spun in the air like pollen.

Inside, another procession was forming.

"Her orbital floors," Emilee murmured. "They're crushed inward. Not from a dashboard." She paused, remembering a case from California—a schoolteacher beaten by a student. "That's deliberate."

Sarah nodded, eyes fixed on the X-ray. "And the occipital plate—flattened. Like her head was pressed into something. Repeatedly."

Before Emilee could respond, a commotion erupted in the hallway.

Scott had gone to the bathroom. Now he was surrounded—three men in black jackets, earpieces glinting under the fluorescents.

Sarah stepped out first. Emilee followed.

At the center of the cluster stood Governor Washman, Scott's father. Former governor. Former everything. Now campaigning for President. He pulled Scott into a hug, firm and practiced.

The governor glanced at Sarah. A flicker of recognition. No warmth.

She knew that look. He'd never forgiven her for walking out on Scott all those years ago.

"Come on," the governor said, resting a hand on his son's shoulder. "Let's grab a bite. There's nothing you can do right now."

Scott hesitated. Then nodded.

The governor turned to Sarah. "You should join us."

She glanced back at Rebecca's room. Then followed.

Two minutes later, a man in scrubs entered Room 3A. He moved quickly, quietly. Checked the chart. Adjusted the I.V. Left without a word.

Rebecca coded.

The monitor flatlined.

The nurse on duty stepped in, saw the red armband.

DNR.

She checked the chart. Verified. Called the time.

19:53

No alarms. No resuscitation. No calls to family.

Just silence.

Then another team arrived—blue jackets, white gloves. They spoke in clipped tones.

"Timing for retrieval?"

"Confirmed. Organs viable."

They wheeled Rebecca's body onto a gurney. Draped a ceremonial flag across her chest—white with a blue flame. The symbol of donation.

As they pushed her down the hallway, staff began to gather. Nurses. Orderlies. Techs.

They clapped.

An honor walk.

Outside, the parade was still going—horns blaring, flags waving, cheers rising into the night.

Inside, no one in the family was informed.

No one knew.

INT. ICU ROOM – EMPTY – NIGHT

The machines were silent. The bed stripped. The lightboard dark.

A single I.V. bag hung from the pole.

Lot number: 2:23495896 Sticker: Purple. a colon.

No one saw it.

CHAPTER 38 - CLASS ACTION

The gymnasium tickled the senses with old varnish and folding chairs. Fluorescent lights buzzed overhead. A banner hung crooked behind the podium: "Public Accountability Forum Trinity General Hospital Practices." The meeting just started minutes before, and it is already heated.

Moderator: "We ask that all comments remain respectful and constructive."

A voice from the crowd shouts out, "Respectful? You called it a 'containment lapse.' My nephew was sedated for three days without consent. That's not a lapse—it's a cover-up."

Moderator: "I understand emotions are high. I was told that the department is reviewing all procedures—"

Audience Member: "You mean rewriting them to sound less criminal?"

Tommy's sister sat in the front row, flanked by Ms. Delaney and two former patients. The crowd overflowed into the hallway—survivors, families, press, and a few staff members who came in plain clothes. At the podium stood Brian Bradley, the lawyer representing Tommy's family and a couple others.

He adjusted the mic. His voice was steady. "This is not a press conference. This is not a PR exercise. This is a town hall, and tonight, we speak plainly."

He gestured to a stack of affidavits and handwritten notes. "These are real accounts. From real people. About real harm. You'll hear them in their own words."

A woman in row three stood up. "They killed my husband back in 2022."

A man near the exit added, "My friend went in with appendicitis. They put him on a respirator. He was dead in hours."

An older woman said, "Grandma was healthy. Went in for a UTI. Never came out."

A younger man spoke next. "my Dad went in with the flu. Discharged with an infection. Brought him back he died within the hour I overheard nurses talking about his yield"

Brian Bradley nodded solemnly. "These are not isolated. These are patterns, and they demand investigation."

A woman in her late seventies stood slowly, gripping the back of her chair for balance. Her voice was steady, but her eyes were glassy.

"My husband and I weren't feeling well. This was during the height of COVID. We went to the ER together. They separated us immediately."

She paused.

"They told me I had a cold bug. No COVID but, he tested positive. I didn't understand. We ate together. Slept together. How could one of us have it and the other not?"

She looked down at her hands.

"They said visiting hours were limited. Fifteen minutes a day. So, I went in. He was heavily medicated. Couldn't speak. Just stared at me."

Her voice cracked.

"I came back the next day. And the next. And the day after that. Every time, he looked worse. Gaunt. Dark circles under his eyes. They had him on the COVID protocol, but I noticed something missing."

She looked up.

"He's diabetic. He wasn't getting his insulin."

Gasps rippled through the crowd.

"I told the nurse. She nodded. Said she'd check. Next day, still no insulin. I asked again. She brushed me off. I asked to speak to someone in administration."

She took a breath.

"I got Delaney. She gave me legal jargon. Liability language. No resolution."

She wiped her eyes.

"I called our family doctor back in Arizona. He said get him out. Get him transferred to St. Louis. I started the paperwork. Told the nurses. They said they'd help."

Her voice dropped.

"I came back the next morning at seven. Ready to pack his things. Ready to bring him home."

She looked at Brian Bradley.

"He wasn't in the room."

The room was silent.

"I asked where he was. A nurse said, 'Oh, he passed last night.' Just like that. My husband of fifty years. Gone."

She sat down slowly.

No one spoke.

Brian Bradley stepped forward, voice low.

"This is what happens when systems lose their soul. When protocols replace people. When silence becomes policy."

A woman in a navy-blue blouse stood near the center aisle. Her voice was calm, but her eyes were fierce.

"My husband was a retired Navy SEAL. Strongest man I ever knew. He survived deployments, injuries, surgeries but, he didn't survive Trinity."

She held up a folder, thick with papers.

"He went in for dehydration. That's all. He was tired, lightheaded. They admitted him overnight for observation."

She opened the folder.

"Within 48 hours, they gave him a flu vaccine—without authorization. He never consented. I never consented."

She flipped a page.

"Then came the meds. I printed the list. I want you to hear it."

She began reading, slow and deliberate:

- "Lorazepam. Twice. No psych history."
- "Haloperidol. For 'agitation.' He was asleep."
- "Zyprexa. Antipsychotic. No diagnosis."
- "Diphenhydramine. Max dose."
- "Morphine. No pain complaint."
- "Fentanyl patch. No record of pain management consult."
- "Midazolam. Twice. No sedation order."
- "Flu vaccine. No consent."
- "Hydroxyzine. For anxiety. He wasn't anxious."
- "Ativan. Again."
- "Seroquel. Again."
- "Trazodone. For sleep. He was already unconscious."

She looked up.

"They sedated him into silence. They drugged him into compliance. They turned a warrior into a patient. Then into a body."

The room was silent.

"I asked for his records. They gave me a summary. I printed the portal logs before and after. They don't match."

She closed the folder.

"They said he died peacefully but, I saw the bruises. I saw the restraints. I saw the fear in his eyes before the meds took him."

She sat down.

Brian Bradley stepped forward, voice low.

"This is not care. This is chemical restraint. This is unauthorized sedation. This is a violation of everything medicine is supposed to protect."

One by one they started to speak . . .

A woman in the back rose. "I truly believe they killed my mother for her organs. She had a donor card."

A man in a veteran's cap stated, "My wife died last night. They already shipped her off for her organs."

A young woman, visibly shaken, spoke next. "My friend was declared brain dead. His sister barged into the OR and stopped the surgery. He was alive."

Brian Bradley leaned forward. "This is why we need independent autopsy access. Chain-of-custody reform, and full transparency on donor protocols."

A woman with a cane added, "They wouldn't give me my usual meds. They gave me things I said no to. Just put it in my IV."

A young mother spoke next. "My husband was clean for ten

years. They treated him like a junkie because of old records."

Brian Bradley's voice sharpened. "This is medical battery. This is diagnostic negligence. This is abuse."

An older veteran stood. "They bilked the VA for every dime. Then kept billing after my brother died."

A woman in the front row said, "They put my husband in as a psych case just to get him seen faster. He ended up locked away for a week."

A former employee added, "I worked for Lakewood. Trinity may be the new name, but the game never changed. It's all about money and accolades."

Brian Bradley tapped the podium. "We're tracking billing fraud. Insurance manipulation, and coercive categorization."

A woman in the back, voice cracking, said, "I tried to hire an attorney. I went to three. No one would help me."

A man holding a folder added, "I had it investigated. The hospital swept it under the rug."

A young woman said, "No lawyer would take the case in Rockford County. They said it wasn't winnable."

Brian Bradley stepped forward. "That's why we will move it out of this county, We're here to break the silence. To build the case. To demand change."

Ms. Delaney rose from her seat. "My grandfather built the Delaney Wing. My father prosecuted in this county. I know what justice looks like, and this isn't it."

Murmurs. Boos. A few tears. Brian Bradley stepped back to the podium, his voice steady but sharp.

"I want to close this meeting with the lawsuit filed today in Rockford County by a woman we are calling *Mrs. X*. For her protection. Because threats have been made against her life and safety for daring to speak the truth."

He held up a thick folder.

"Online astroturfers—posing as medical experts—have tried to discredit her. Blogs, comment threads, even fake websites but, what I'm about to read is not speculation. It is not theory. It is the truth."

He opened the folder.

"Based on medical notes and summaries pulled directly from Trinity General's patient portal, Mr. X— did not have MRSA, sepsis, or pneumonia. His primary issue was acute hypoxic respiratory failure caused by fluid around the heart and a dangerously low ejection fraction."

He looked up.

"Despite this, Trinity administered a cocktail of medications—many of which were not only unnecessary, but suspiciously aligned with organ preservation protocols."

He began to read.

1. Overuse of Antibiotics

Vancomycin, Cefepime, Ciprofloxacin, Piperacillin/Tazobactam, Azithromycin

"These were given to treat infections he didn't have. Why? Because broad-spectrum antibiotics suppress bacterial growth and reduce the risk of contamination—ideal conditions for organ harvesting."

2. Excessive Sedation and Anesthesia

Propofol, Midazolam, Lorazepam, Precedex, Etomidate

"These drugs suppress respiratory drive and induce coma-like states. In harvesting protocols, they're used to keep the body quiet—to reduce movement, reduce oxygen demand, and preserve organ viability."

3. Cardiovascular Strain from Vasopressors and Antiarrhythmics

Amiodarone, Diltiazem, Levophed, Midodrine

"These drugs can stabilize blood pressure—but in excess, they strain the heart. They're often used to maintain perfusion long enough to keep organs viable, even as the heart fails."

4. Electrolyte Replacement Therapies

Potassium Chloride, Magnesium Sulfate, Sodium Phosphate

"Electrolyte correction is standard—but aggressive replacement can mask organ distress. It's also used to optimize cellular conditions for transplant."

5. Psychiatric Medications and Agitation Management

Haldol, Seroquel, Trazodone, Valproate Sodium

"These were given despite no psychiatric diagnosis. Why? Because sedation reduces resistance. These drugs are used to quiet patients, suppress complaints, and chemically restrain."

6. Opioids and Pain Management

Fentanyl, Morphine, OxyContin

"Powerful opioids depress respiration. In harvesting protocols, they're used to reduce metabolic activity and ease the transition to brain death."

7. Unnecessary Vaccination and Eye Drops

Flu vaccine, artificial tears

"He was given a flu vaccine without consent. Why vaccinate a dying man? Because it reduces viral load in harvested tissue. Artificial tears were administered—standard in donor prep to prevent corneal drying."

Bradley paused.

"These medications weren't just excessive. They were strategic."

He flipped to the final page.

"Mr. X died four months later but, the damage was done in the first 48 hours. His heart failed. His kidneys failed. His lungs collapsed. And Trinity called it 'complications.'"

He looked out at the crowd.

"We call it what it is: medical battery. Diagnostic fraud. And premeditated harvesting."

He stepped back from the mic.

"We will not be gaslit. We will not be buried in euphemism. We will not be quiet.

Trinity General Hospital —your reckoning begins tonight."

CHAPTER 39 – ASTROTURF

Within 16 minutes of the story breaking on Channel 3, Sarah Hart's inbox was flooded.

Not with praise. Not with tips.

With accusations.

"Disgraced detective pushes conspiracy theory."

"Hart's vendetta against Trinity General rooted in personal bias."

"Former officer with history of misconduct now targeting healthcare heroes."

Many headlines, each one more polished than the last. Same tone. Same phrasing. Different outlets.

Some were local blogs she'd never heard of. Others were national platforms with suspiciously similar layouts—stock photos, vague credentials, no bylines.

The comments were worse.

"She's just bitter she got passed over."

"This is what happens when you let unstable women play cop."

"She's exploiting veterans for attention."

Sarah didn't flinch. She'd seen this playbook before.

Astroturfing.

A coordinated campaign to make lies look like grassroots truth.

Manufactured outrage.

Fake experts.

Paid trolls.

All designed to drown the signal in noise.

She clicked through the articles. One cited a "former colleague" who claimed Sarah had falsified reports.

Another quoted an anonymous "hospital source" who said she'd harassed staff.

None of it was true.

But truth didn't trend.

She opened her laptop and ran a reverse image search on one of the "experts" quoted in three separate pieces. The photo was a stock model—used in an ad for arthritis cream.

She checked the domain registration on one of the sites. It had been created two days ago. The IP address traced back to a PR firm in St. Louis.

Sarah traces the PR firm linking them to Trinity donors

They were ready for me, she thought. They knew this was coming.

Her phone buzzed. A message from Willie.

They're trying to bury you. Stay loud. Stay clean.

Sarah smiled, just barely.

She opened her notes, pulled up the intake logs, the coded I.V. bags, the sticker system, the metadata. She had the chain of custody. She had the names.

And she had the truth.

She wasn't going to fight the lies one by one.

She was going to drown them in evidence.

CHAPTER 40- THE WOODS

The woods behind the veterans shelter were quiet, but not peaceful. The trees stood like sentinels. Sarah stepped carefully over roots and fallen limbs, clutching the rolled diagrams in her arms. The wind carried the scent of damp earth and distant smoke.

She found Marcus—beneath the collapsed lean-to near the creek bed, half-hidden by brush and shadow. He was sharpening a piece of rebar into a makeshift tool, his hands steady. "I brought the schematics," Sarah stated, kneeling beside him.

Marcus looked up slowly. His face was drawn, but alert. He wiped his hands on his coat and took the papers from her. She spread them out on a flat rock: the Hospital layout, the city hall diagram, and the underground waterways. Each one marked, circled, annotated in red.

"Could there be sub-levels?" she asked.

Marcus didn't answer right away. He traced a line on the Hospital layout with his finger, then tapped a section labeled Transfer Line 3A. "I've seen them," he stated. "That's how they move people. Underground. Quiet. Fast."

Sarah leaned closer. The conduit ran beneath both Trinity General Hospital and City Hall, connecting to storm drains and maintenance shafts. It had been buried—literally and bureaucratically. "They're trafficking people," she realized. "Not just patients—kids, runaways, anyone they think won't be missed?"

Marcus's jaw tightened. He flipped to the map of the waterways, pointing to a section marked *Inactive*. It was a lie. He'd seen movement there. Vans. Stretchers. Men in scrubs who didn't work at any Hospital . "It's bigger than I could've ever imagined," he admitted. "I thought it was just the Hospital , but this—this is infrastructure."

Sarah traced the map with her finger. The lines weren't just routes—they were veins. The town was bleeding people, and no one had noticed. "We need to get inside," she stated. "Document everything. Names. Faces. Routes."

Marcus nodded. "We'll need gear. Masks. Flashlights, and I'll need a gun

Sarah folded the maps carefully, her hands trembling. "Let's go," she said.

CHAPTER 41 - DEEP DIVE

The drive out of town was quiet. Marcus looked out the window as they drove past the edge of town. The neon faded, replaced by dense thickets of oak and sassafras. A doe stood at the roadside, ribs showing through patchy fur, eyes glassy in the moonlight.

Kudzu climbed the telephone poles like it was trying to choke the wires. In the distance, he saw a flash of movement—maybe a fox, maybe something else. The woods didn't care who you were. They swallowed everything the same.

Sarah kept her eyes on the road. Neither of them spoke until the neon sign of a roadside motel flickered into view. She pulled into the gravel lot and parked beneath a broken streetlamp. The air smelled like rain and gasoline.

Inside, the room was small but clean. Marcus dropped his bag and headed for the shower without a word. Sarah sat at the desk, opened her laptop, and began to dig.

She started with the state's juvenile detention centers. The numbers were staggering. Thousands of entries marked *escapee*, *AWOL*, *runaway*. She cross-referenced with child services. The language was softer, but the numbers were worse. "Runaways," she muttered. "Lost in the system."

She pulled up the most recent annual report. Her eyes scanned the page, then froze. 13,482 children reported missing from state care in the last calendar year. That wasn't a spike. That was a tell. The detention centers called them escapees. Child services called them runaways.

Then she cross-referenced with organ procurement data. Legal pediatric donors in the U.S. are typically between 11 and 17 years old. The overlap was grotesque. The same age range. The same invisibility. The same systems that failed to protect them now quietly processed their bodies for "viable outcomes." She whispered it aloud, just to hear it in the room: **"They're harvesting ghost**s."

Marcus stepped out of the bathroom, towel around his shoulders, steam trailing behind him. "You need to see this," Sarah said. He sat beside her, still damp.

She pulled up the latest detention intake report for Rockford County. This year alone, 614 juveniles were processed. Of those, 47 were marked as "escapees." That was nearly 8%—a figure that didn't match the official tone of "isolated incidents."

"Forty-seven escapees. From one county. In one year."

Marcus looked at the numbers again. **"That's not just failure,"** he said. **"That's supply."**

Sarah nodded. "They're feeding the underground corridors."

Marcus stood and pulled the maps from his bag. He spread them across the bed. He grabbed a tourist map of The Belt Buckle of the Bible Belt from the motel's welcome binder and uncapped a marker. "I've walked these," he stated. He began to draw—lines snaking beneath streets, connecting buildings.

Sarah circled buildings: the courthouse, the child services office, Trinity General Hospital , the old juvenile intake center. Marcus marked each building with an X. The tunnel map matched the X's. Every building had a conduit beneath it. Every conduit had a purpose.

"They're not just connected," Sarah realized. "They're

coordinated."

Marcus stared at the maps, his eyes dark. "Each building must have access," he stated. "From inside. That's how they move people without anyone seeing."

Sarah spread another blueprint across the table. Near the southeast quadrant, she paused. "What's that?" she asked, pointing to a rounded shape.

"Retention pond," Marcus replied automatically.

"It's not a pond," she stated. She used a magnifying glass. "Look—there's framing beneath. Reinforced walls. Vents."

Marcus squinted. "That's substructure. Buried."

Just below the shape, in smudged ink: 15:4.

Sarah grabbed the bible on the nightstand.

She exhaled. "Luke 15:4: 'What man of you, having a hundred sheep, if he loses one of them, doth not leave the ninety and nine in the wilderness, and go after that which is lost, until he finds it?' The lost sheep. They marked it. Not for drainage. For disappearance."

Marcus circled the area with his pen. "Then that's where we go."

Sarah looked at the numbers again. Thirteen thousand kids. Hundreds of adults. Dozens of buildings. "This isn't a town," she stated. "It's a machine."

Marcus nodded. "And we just found the gears."

CHAPTER 42 - THE TUNNELS

Incoming Text:

"Where the cold waits for silence, follow the hum."

Emilee stared at it for a long time, heart thudding. It wasn't the first cryptic message she'd received but, this one felt different—it wasn't just a clue but a warning.

She waited until her shift ended, then doubled back through the east corridor. Past the laundry chute. Past the old radiology wing. Down the stairwell the air was engulfed with bleach .

The basement was quiet.

She passed the storage cages, the broken gurneys, the forgotten wheelchairs. The morgue door loomed ahead—unmarked, but unmistakable.

Inside, refrigerated and still. The hum of the compressor was the only sound.

She moved past the body drawers, past the autopsy table, toward the far wall. There, behind a row of stacked linens, she found it: a narrow metal door, painted the same dull gray as the wall. No handle. Just a keypad.

She took a wild guess and entered **223**. Nothing happened so she entered 99

The door clicked open.

A tunnel.

Concrete walls. Low ceiling. Just wide enough to walk through without turning sideways. It was damp, but not foul, more like dust and old paper.

She didn't have to go far.

Just fifty feet in, the tunnel opened into a junction—four paths, each marked only by the direction they led.

One tunnel curved back toward the morgue.

Another stretched straight ahead, ending in a wide loading bay with a roll-up door. The concrete was scuffed with tire marks. The ceiling was high enough to back in a semi-truck.

The third tunnel veered left, narrower but lit by a single overhead bulb. At the far end sat a golf cart with a four-wheel trailer attached. The trailer was empty, but the floor beneath it was stained.

Air scraped past Emilee's clenched teeth. This was how they did it.

No paperwork. No witnesses. No alarms.

Bodies were moved from the morgue into the tunnel. Loaded onto the cart. Driven to the bay. Transferred to trucks. No one above ground ever saw a thing.

She pulled out her phone and started filming The cart. The trailer.

She didn't know how long she had before someone noticed she was missing.

But she knew one thing:

She wasn't leaving without proof.

Another text

Code

Orange walks to sacred ground,

Where graves are stacked and prayers are drowned.

Green is sold where shadows keep,

The market waits for those who sleep.

Purple marks the body's trade,

Not fit to gift, but parts are paid.

And black forbids the hand to take,

For breaking this would wake the snake.

Her throat tightened. She whispered the lines aloud, testing them against one of Natalie's notes

Emilee couldn't stop seeing the stickers. Orange. Green. Purple. They clung to her thoughts like bruises. She'd written them in her notebook, circled them, underlined them, but the meaning stayed just out of reach.

Until now.

Natalie's note read:

- Orange → sacred ground. The old church cemetery.

Emilee had heard rumors of tunnels beneath Trinity leading there.

- Green → sold in shadows. The warehouse district. Trafficking.
- Purple → the body's trade. Cadavers, tissue, blood. Nothing wasted to Delaney airfield.
- Black → forbidden. VIPs, protected patients. "Wake the snake"—Crawford's warning.

Her hand shook as she copied the riddle into her notebook.

The colored stickers weren't just markers. They were routing codes.

A subway map for the dead. She needed to get to Sarah, Sarah needed to know before she went any further.

She turned back toward the junction, heart pounding.

This wasn't just a clue.

It was a supply chain.

She pulled out her phone and started filming—quietly, methodically. The tire marks. The roll-up door.

Then she opened her contacts and tapped Sarah's name.

The phone rang once.

Twice.

She pressed it tighter to her ear

The light flickered.

A sound behind her.

Not footsteps.

Not a voice.

Just a shift in the air.

She turned.

Everything went black.

CHAPTER 43 – TAKEN

The motel room was hushed, lit only by the glow of Sarah's laptop and the soft purr of the heater. Marcus had fallen asleep on the second bed; maps still spread across the comforter like a crime scene. Sarah was reviewing intake records again when her phone buzzed. Incoming Call: Emilee. Sarah was just getting out of the shower, the phone rang a second time

Her breath caught. She finally answered "Emilee?"

Silence. Sarah waited, her heart pounding. She was about to hang up when she heard it—a whisper. Faint. Then two male voices, low and muffled, speaking over each other. She couldn't make out the words, but the tone was urgent. Rough. Not medical.

She put the call on speaker. Marcus stirred, sat up, listening. "They've got her," he whispered.

The call cut off. Sarah tried calling back. Straight to voicemail. Her fingers trembling. She dialed Alvarez. He picked up on the second ring.

"Detective Alvarez."

"It's Sarah. I think Emilee's in danger. Possibly taken. I just got a call from her number—there were men's voices. She didn't speak."

There was a pause. Then a chuckle. "Sarah, I think you watch too many crime dramas."

Silence. Sarah didn't respond. She looked at Marcus. He was

already shaking his head. The corruption went that deep. "He's in on it," she muttered. Alvarez's voice kept talking, something about protocol and false alarms, but Sarah had stopped listening. She hung up.

Marcus stood, pulling the maps off the bed. "We move now," he stated. "Before they disappear her for good."

Sarah nodded, already packing. The motel room felt smaller now. Like the walls were listening.

Marcus and Sarah didn't speak as they sped down the highway toward Rockford County. The silence between them was loaded. Sarah's knuckles were white on the steering wheel. Marcus stared out the window, scanning every passing car.

They pulled into the Hospital lot just after sunrise. The building loomed, sterile and indifferent. Sarah parked crookedly and jumped out.

Inside, the shift board showed Emilee's name—but no check-in. Sarah approached the front desk. "Has anyone seen Emilee?" she demanded. "Emilee Vaughn. She was supposed to work last night."

The nurse looked up, confused. "She didn't show. No call. No message."

Sarah's stomach dropped. She checked the staff lounge. Emilee's locker was empty. There was no discharge note. No movement record. Just an empty locker. Emilee hadn't left. She'd been removed. Her badge was gone. Her phone went straight to voicemail.

Marcus met her in the hallway, eyes grim. "She's not here."

Sarah felt a chill crawl down her spine. She opened her notebook and added Emilee's name to the list. The list of the taken. She clenched her fists. "Then we go back into the underground passages," she asserted. "And we don't come out until we find her."

Marcus nodded. "They'll move her through Conduit C3. No cameras, no logs. I know the route. That's how we will find her."

CHAPTER 44 – THE HUNT BEGINS

Rain is pouring down even though its day, its dark. Roy drove Marcus and Sarah through the back streets of old Rockford County, past shuttered storefronts and rusted playgrounds.

They stopped at a crumbling building near the edge of town. Sarah's flashlight beam caught graffiti spray-painted in deep BLUE across the back wall: "99 LEFT BEHIND" Beneath it, a smaller line in black: Luke 15:4.

"It's scripture," she recalled. "The parable of the lost sheep. 'If one is missing, won't you leave the ninety-nine to find it?'"

Marcus nodded slowly. "Or mark where they were taken."

Roy stayed back. "That tag's been there since '19. It's how they signaled safe entry points. For transfers. For extraction. For anyone who knew what to look for."

Marcus adjusted his backpack. "Then this is where we begin."

Roy reached under the dash and pulled out a manila envelope. "Here," he said. "This is everything I know."

Inside: a transportation log Roy had kept in the van, and a marked-up tunnel map. Red ink traced the paths. Blue circles marked vents. Black X's for dead ends. In the corner, three initials: **SMH**.

Roy took the map and grabbed a yellow highlighter. "Listen," he stated, voice low. "With this rain, it's going to be chaos down there. Some of the sub-levels will be full of drainage—fast, unpredictable."

He marked a long curve. "This conduit here—it's high ground. If you try to cut through this section"—he tapped a cluster of red lines— "you'll get swept up. No question."

Marcus nodded, took the map back, and handed the ledger to Sarah.

And just like that, the rain stopped. The stillness felt sudden. Heavy.

Roy looked toward the hospital in the distance, then back at Marcus. "You've got one shot," he stated. "Make it count."

Roy reached into his coat pocket and held out a small brass compass. "Take this," he said. "GPS won't work down there. Too much concrete."

Marcus took it. "You sure you don't want to come?"

Roy shook his head. "I've done enough damage, but I can still point the way."

Sarah looked up. "You really think she's still in there?"

Roy didn't answer right away. "Honestly? I don't know if anyone could survive that place," he admitted. He paused. "But I've seen miracles before. I experienced one in Kandahar. You saved us."

Marcus said nothing, just tucked the compass into his jacket.

Roy looked at Sarah. "God works in mysterious ways If anyone can get through that place and come back with the truth—it's him."

Marcus looked at the map. "I've always hated that saying!

Ok, then let's go."

CHAPTER 45 – INFILTRATION

The windows were boarded up, the front door chained. Marcus didn't hesitate. He pulled a magnet and a lighter from his jacket. These were not locks to be picked; they were targets for remote defeat, a specialty of his combat engineer training. He angled the paint can using the magnet. "Improvised breach charge," he muttered, describing the physics as he lit the wick. "Standard field-expedient application."

He used the magnet to hold the paint can, angled the nozzle, and inserted the flyer wick. He lit the wick. The flame hissed. Marcus stepped back, shielding Sarah. The can burst with a sharp, concussive pop. The padlock cracked sideways.

"Boom enough," he muttered.

He led her around to the basement entrance, where a rusted metal hatch sat half-buried in weeds. "This used to be a shelter," he explained. "Now it's a drop point."

Sarah followed him down. The basement was dark and damp. Their flashlights cut through the dust, revealing scattered 'Wells Supply' medical supplies—I.V. bags, syringes, patient wristbands.

Marcus crouched by Roy's map. He wasn't just memorizing the layout—he was calculating steam lines, pressure valves, electrical junctions. He traced them with his finger. "Boiler surge here," he muttered. "That's a pressure choke. If it backs up, it'll blow sideways." This was the knowledge he gained mapping subterranean threats—how heat warped metal, how pressure moved through unstable systems. He was reading the infrastructure like a threat assessment report.

a flow of sewage-feeding insects

Sarah glanced over. "You think we'll need to reroute?"

"I think we'll need to improvise," he said.

He pulled a rewired penlight from his jacket. "You learn to make do. I'm saying I know how things break, and how to make that happen on purpose."

Behind a rusted boiler, Marcus pulled back a panel.

A conduit stretched into the earth—narrow, silent, and terrifying. The air inside was damp, metallic. The walls were concrete, lined with old wiring and rusted brackets.

The air was colder here.

Sarah crouched low, flashlight sweeping across the concrete floor. The tunnel had narrowed, then opened into a junction—four paths, each marked by a painted symbol above its entrance. The walls were damp, the silence thick.

Marcus stood behind her, one hand on the rusted boiler panel he'd pried open.

"Wonder what that all means."

Sarah didn't hesitate. She pulled a folded paper from her coat pocket—Natalie's note, copied and passed through Emilee's hands like a lifeline.

"I know," she said. "Well… Natalie knew."

She held it up to the light. The handwriting was shaky but deliberate.

- Green for the living—sold in shadows.

- Purple for the harvested—taken off the street.
- Orange for the buried—evidence erased.

She pointed to each tunnel in turn.

The green square marked the widest tunnel, leading toward the warehouse district. The concrete was worn smooth, like it had seen wheels and boots and silence.

"Trafficking," Sarah said. "The ones they sell. Sex trade. Rituals."

The purple circle marked a narrower path, veering toward the industrial zone.

"Harvesting," Marcus added. "The ones taken off the street. Not profitable alive, but valuable in pieces."

The orange triangle was painted above a tunnel that sloped downward, toward the old church cemetery.

"Burials," Sarah said. "The ones they erase. Evidence. Bodies. Anything that didn't pass the sort."

Then Sarah turned to the fourth tunnel.

It was newer. Cleaner. A yellow diamond gleamed above the entrance.

She frowned.

"Yellow wasn't in Natalie's note."

Marcus looked at his map ran his finger across it and pointed. He stepped forward, voice low.

"That one leads to the courthouse. And the holding cells. Juvenile detention."

Sarah's breath folded inward.

"They're pulling from the jail?"

Marcus nodded.

"According to the map, yeah. That's where yellow goes."

Sarah turned back to the purple tunnel, her pulse rising.

"They won't take Emilee through orange—she's not dead. Not yet."

"And not green," Marcus said. "She knows too much. They wouldn't risk her talking."

Sarah's voice dropped.

"Then it's purple. They'll harvest her."

Marcus didn't speak.

He didn't have to.

Sarah gripped her flashlight tighter; eyes locked on the tunnel.

"We have to move. Now."

They followed the marked path. The air grew colder. The walls narrowed. They reached a steel door in the middle of this tunnel with a keypad—unmarked, industrial. Marcus knelt beside it.

The chain around his neck clinked—dog tags, a worn silver cross, and a slim, rectangular chip embedded in the pendant. "She told me once," he whispered, "some staff wore dual-ID tags for access. One for protocol. This cross was her second ID. I was here years ago, but never made it past this door."

He slid the cross into the narrow slot beneath the keypad. A soft green light blinked. Marcus then typed a six-digit code—the kind you remember because someone begged you to.

The lock clicked. The door quietly released.

Marcus stood, eyes hard. "She wanted me to find this."

Sarah reached for his arm. "Then let's find her."

Inside was a small room—bare walls, a single cot, a camera mounted in the corner. It reeked of urine, antiseptic, and fear. "They must hold people here before transport," Marcus surmised.

Sarah stepped inside. There were initials carved into the wall. Names. Dates. Messages. *"Still here." "Don't forget me."* The letters "T R". She pointed at the initials. "Tommy Reynolds?" she questioned.

"I don't know, but maybe?" Marcus admitted with a low, sad tone.

She took photos of every carving. "We need more than pictures," she stated. "We need to find Emilee."

This room was a dead end. Marcus led Sarah out and back down the underground passages. The air was damp and cold; the walls lined with old pipes.

"You know, Natalie was my wife, she called me," Hayes said, sensing Hart's quiet focus. "Said something felt wrong at the Hospital —like people were disappearing." He paused. "I drove all night to get here, but by the time I arrived, she was already GONE. No explanation. No warning. Just… GONE." He inhaled slowly. "That's when I started digging, and I haven't stopped since."

After miles of winding paths—hallways that looped like they were designed to disorient—they reached a dead end. The air was thick with mildew, every breath tasting of rust and rot. His prosthetic socket had begun to chafe hours ago, the damp seeping in and turning each step into a grind of skin against carbon and steel.

The slick concrete forced him to shorten his stride; his balance tested with every uneven patch. Sweat stung his eyes, but it was the dull, insistent ache where flesh met machine that gnawed at his focus. He shifted his weight, listening to the faint echo of dripping water, the scurry of rats in unseen channels, and the hollow thud of his own footfall—one sound organic, the other metallic, both reminders of how far he'd come and how little margin for error remained.

Marcus pulled out the map Roy had handed him when he dropped them off. The edges were soft from folding; the ink smudged in places. He traced the lines with his thumb.

"This is it," he whispered.

He used the cross again on this keypad on this door and it worked. They emerged into a narrow utility closet—walls lined with rusted shelving, coils of wire, and a mop that hadn't been used in years. A lingering whiff that was thick with ammonia and something older. Something that clawed at your nasal passage like rats, cooler ice and bleach that never quite masked the rot.

Scaffolding and broken pallets boxed them in. Half-dead fluorescent bulbs blinked overhead, casting the space in a stuttering light. The floor was uneven—grime layered over concrete, patches of standing water that registered the odor of metal.

They passed three dead mice. One had curled into itself like it had tried to hide.

Marcus scanned for movement. His Marine Corps training surfaced immediately—angles, shadows, exits. Every sharp tang of metal or mildew hit him with the force of memory. The prosthetic made his steps deliberate, measured. He'd learned to move without sound, even when the world beneath him wasn't built for it.

Sarah stepped lightly beside him, eyes sharp, breath steady.

Somewhere ahead, the murmur of a cooler unit pulsed through the walls.

They weren't alone.

Sarah bent down and pulled a secondary pistol from her boot, handing it to him.

Marcus took it with a flicker of relief. His fingers curled around the grip like they'd been waiting for it.

Hart's own weapon, drawn from her waist, was already held ready.

They moved forward.

He stepped over a collapsed shelving unit, his prosthetic clunking. Sarah moved ahead, flashlight sweeping the walls. "This place wasn't built for patients," she whispered. "It was built to hide them."

The distant humming sharpened, drawing them to a new steel door, reinforced and sealed with a biometric pad. Marcus pressed the cross from his neck chain to the reader. A green light blinked twice. The lock didn't click.

Sarah stepped forward and kicked the door hard. It groaned open, cold air rushing out like a tomb's breath.

Inside, everything changed. The room was pristine. White walls, surgical lights, and stainless-steel trays gleamed. Monitors hummed softly.

At the room's center, a figure lay splayed out on an operating table, wrists strapped. It was Emilee.

Beside her, a tall figure in a white medical jacket hovered. His gloved hand held a scalpel, the silver blade trembling at the edge of Emilee's exposed skin.

Marcus staggered. Rage heated his chest, but his years had taught him control.

"Dr. Crawford, step away from her," Sarah called, her voice sharp and fire-edged. The barrel of her gun cut an arc between them.

Crawford jerked, eyes wild. The scalpel fell, sparking off the concrete.

Marcus moved instantly, his prosthetic clunking as he reached Emilee. Her hands, pinched and trembling, slid free under his touch.

"Emilee! Are you all right?" his whisper cracked.

"I—I think so," she managed, small and broken. "Are there others?"

Sarah kept her position, eyes never leaving Crawford. Hayes's gut twisted. The cost of Emilee's faith was written in the marks on her skin and the terror in her eyes. The alliance between the veteran and the detective was forged in shared danger—a shield against the monsters in lab coats.

Emilee grabbed his forearm. "Please. Don't let him go," she whispered.

But Crawford's shuffling drew his attention. In a sliver of movement, Crawford pushed over a stack of pallets that thundered down toward Sarah. He then lunged for the far side—a door burst open, and he slipped into the darkness beyond.

The door snapped closed, swallowing him whole. Marcus slammed his weight forward, pain flaring through his joints. He glanced down at Sarah, who was getting up from the floor. She motioned for him to go after Crawford.

CHAPTER 46 – GODS HOUSE

As soon as he got through the door, the scene changed from sterile to filthy.

The warehouse stretched in front of him—rows of rusted shelving and splintered pallets, the sharp scent of motor oil and mold stinging his nose as he tore ahead. Somewhere up ahead, Crawford's footsteps clattered over broken glass and sheet metal, quick and desperate.

Marcus darted behind a leaning crate, his boot slipping on a patch of oily concrete. The prosthetic skidded, metal scraping against the floor with a hollow clack. Every stride fired a jag of agony up his thigh, but he pressed on. The veteran's senses ran three steps ahead; the warehouse felt alive.

Sarah's voice snapped through the dark, steady and urgent. "He's heading back to the tunnels!"

Her call hung in the shadows, chased by the hiss of her radio and the echo of retreating footsteps.

He needed a faster way to the tunnels.

Marcus spotted the hatch—low to the ground, half-concealed beneath a rusted dolly and a torn sheet of insulation. He dropped to one knee, gritting his teeth as the stump flared. The hatch was old, industrial, sealed with a recessed latch. He yanked it open with a grunt.

Cool air rushed up from below—damp, metallic, threaded with bleach and rat musk.

He dropped through.

The tunnel swallowed him instantly. Concrete walls pressed close, the ceiling low enough to force a crouch. His boots splashed through standing water. The prosthetic thudded with each step, rhythmic and punishing.

Ahead, the distance between Marcus and the Doctor shrank.

Crawford's hunched form was just visible as he crashed through a flimsy wire fence—a temporary wall giving way to another set of tunnels. Scratching echoed behind him—rats, dozens of them, stirred by movement and scent.

Then a jolt of anger lashed through Marcus's stomach. Not fear. Not duty.

Anger.

He surged forward—faster, lungs scraping, stump screaming, but his drive was bigger. He wasn't chasing Crawford.

He was chasing the truth.

Crawford angled left. Marcus shouldered through after him. The air thickened with the stench of antiseptic and rotting flesh. Surgical gloves, I.V. bags, and a tossed bedpan crunched underfoot. Marcus's boot squelched; the prosthetic rang hollow. He heard Crawford's quick, scraping pant.

Marcus drove himself, heart choking up his throat. He barreled through a narrow section where rusted pipes ran low overhead. He ducked, but a jagged piece of metal—a bent wire tie—caught the chain around his neck. The sudden, brutal resistance slammed his chin forward.

He didn't stop. He couldn't. The chain snapped and ripped free, tearing the dog tags and Natalie's silver cross from his neck.

They clattered against the concrete and sheet metal, spinning and skidding backward into the filth and shadow of the tunnel.

He kept running. His leg throbbed with every stride, the prosthetic hammering against uneven ground but, he was lighter now—stripped of hesitation, severed from the weight of his past. Only the goal remained.

The tunnel narrowed, then angled upward. He climbed, half-stumbling, half-hauling himself toward a sliver of light ahead. The air changed—less damp, more brittle. Dust, not mildew. Stone, not concrete.

Then the smell hit him.

Charred bone. Burnt linen. A chemical sweetness that didn't belong.

He passed through a narrow corridor lined with scorched tiles and rusted trays. Ash clung to the walls. A broken incinerator door hung ajar, its hinges warped. Another unit farther down still hummed faintly—low, mechanical, alive.

A clipboard lay on a hook beside the door. No names. Just codes. Just timestamps.

Marcus gagged, but didn't stop. This wasn't a relic.

It was the final removal.

The walls weren't just scorched—they were used. The ash wasn't just residue—it was routine. Every tray, every warped hinge, every humming unit whispered the same truth: this was where the unrecorded ended. Where the unwanted were erased.

The unused parts processed He pressed forward, lungs burning, leg screaming, heart locked on the man ahead.

He pushed through a warped metal door and emerged into a stone-walled basement—low ceiling, cracked floor, the faint echo of dripping water. Religious pamphlets lay scattered across a folding table. A wooden cross leaned against the wall, half-buried in dust.

He climbed the stairs.

Each step creaked under his weight. The air grew colder, thinner. The silence deepened.

He reached a wooden door and slammed through it.

Light spilled in.

Marcus blinked, chest heaving, and looked up.

A stone archway rose above him, fractured but still standing. The atmosphere was cold, hollow, reverent. He stepped forward.

An old church.

The pews were splintered, some overturned, others missing entirely. Shards of stained glass clung to the windows like broken teeth. Light filtered through in fractured colors—red, blue, gold—casting bruised halos across the floor.

At the far end, the altar still stood. Behind it, the pulpit.

Crawford was there.

Bent. Breathing hard. Framed by the ruins of faith and silence.

Marcus didn't speak.

He lifted the pistol with both hands, his aim steadying on the back of Crawford's head.

"Turn around! Hands where I can see them!" Marcus demanded, his voice rough. "Tell me where the others are—all the patients. Every name."

Crawford turned slowly, hands raised. "You made it," he stated, voice calm. "I was hoping you would." He stepped behind the pulpit. "You know, Marcus, this place was condemned years ago, but I kept it. For moments like this."

Marcus's grip tightened. "You were going to cut her open."

"I was going to save her," Crawford asserted. "Like I've saved dozens. Hundreds."

Marcus's voice cracked. "You call that saving?"

The Doctor leaned forward, eyes gleaming. "Matthew 10:39— 'Whoever finds their life will lose it, and whoever loses their life for my sake will find it.' They don't understand, Marcus. Every day, seventeen people die waiting for an organ. I've saved lives, Marcus."

Marcus stepped closer. "By taking others."

Crawford's voice rose, sermon-like. "John 15:13— 'Greater love hath no man than this, that a man lay down his life for his friends.' They are saints, Marcus. Sacrificed not in vain, but in service. Their bodies become vessels."

Marcus's breath came fast. "You're not God."

"No," The Doctor whispered. "But I am His hands."

"You're done," Marcus repeated.

Crawford smiled again. "You can kill me, but the protocol lives. The saints are already among us."

"I asked you a question," Marcus demanded, his finger flexing on the trigger. "Where are they? Where are the bodies?"

Just then Sarah appeared through the doorway, gun in hand, pointed directly center-mass. Marcus glanced back just for a split second to acknowledge her presence.

Crawford's smile deepened. "You always were persistent, Hayes. It is Hayes, right? Reminds me of someone else." His gaze seemed to slide through Marcus. "I knew a Hayes once: Nat… Natalie. She was persistent like that, too."

The name hit Marcus with the force of a bullet. Crawford smiled, his voice a deliberate cut. "It's never about the missing or the exploited, is it? It's about Natalie. Sweet, sweet Nurse Natalie."

Marcus fought the urge to spit. "Don't," he muttered.

Crawford moved behind the pulpit. "You knew she was special, didn't you? She was willing, Marcus. That's what you never understood. She gave herself. Romans 12:1— 'Present your bodies as a living sacrifice, holy and acceptable to God.' And she was acceptable."

Crawford's voice dropped to a clinical tone. "You know why we don't use the dead, Hayes? Fresh is always better. A living body knows it's dying—it fights you, gives off all the right signals. Even her—she didn't stop until the last moment. That's the price: not just organs, but the moment they cross over."

Marcus's grip tightened, the pistol trembling.

Crawford's eyes gleamed. "And Natalie… she was exquisite. Her body fought, yes, but her soul knew. She gave herself. Like a bride at the altar."

Crawford ignored the gun. "Girlfriends," he stated. "They always say it's about love, but it's vengeance, veteran. You don't want justice. You want me to hurt the way you did that night in the ER."

Marcus jerked his chin up, his voice scraped raw. "She wasn't my girlfriend: she was my PARTNER, my WIFE!"

Crawford's sneer never softened. He leaned forward, voice dropping to a whisper. "I kissed her, Marcus. Just as the last breath left her lips. She tasted like candy."

Something in Marcus broke. The pain, the guilt, the years of silence—all of it surged forward, unstoppable. The pistol felt lighter.

A gunshot shattered the silence.

Crawford slammed backward, mouth twisted, eyes open. Blood pooled fast and black, staining the cracked wood flooring.

Marcus stood frozen, his own unfired pistol still loaded in his hand. He hadn't pulled the trigger.

"ROY!" Emilee's cry echoed through the archway. She was running toward them, pale and frantic.

Marcus and Sarah whirled around. Between them and the newly arrived Emilee stood Roy Hansen, the pistol held steady in his trembling hand, smoke curling from the barrel.

"There was something shiny in his hand," Roy confessed, his voice ragged but resolute. "I thought it was a gun. I thought he was going to shoot you, Marcus."

Marcus's hand shook violently; the pistol he hadn't fired clattering to the ground. Roy had paid the price for them all.

All that could be heard was water leaking, drop by endless drop, masking the sound of shadows that swallowed the room.

CHAPTER 47 – CUFFS

The sirens started as a distant warble—faint enough to ignore, until they grew louder, sharper, undeniable. The woods surrounding the church remained still, but inside, everything was unraveling.

Emilee sat on a pew wrapped in Marcus's Field Jacket. Her hands trembled. Her eyes were glassy, unfocused, but she was awake. Alive. Sarah knelt beside her. "You, ok?" she whispered. "You're safe now ok."

Emilee glanced up, still in shock. "Is your middle name… Marie?" Sarah blinked, then softened. "No. It's Mae." Emilee mouthed the letters anyway—S.M.H.—as if testing them against Sarah's face. The sound of sirens swelled outside, drowning the thought before it could settle.

Marcus stood at the window, staring out into the trees. His posture was rigid, but his mind was far away. He didn't flinch at the sound of approaching engines.

Outside, sirens.

Sarah rose instantly, pulling a pair of handcuffs from her belt. She walked quickly to Roy, whose hands were still raised from dropping the pistol.

"I know, Roy, I'm sorry," she murmured, her voice steady and professional, but heavy with regret. "Chain of custody." She gently placed his hands behind his back and secured the cuffs.

Roy didn't resist. He looked past Sarah, his eyes locking onto

Marcus.

"You saved my life too many times, Gunny," Roy stated, his voice hollow but clear. "That shot wasn't for me, or even for you." He paused, his gaze filled with sorrow for the dead and the disappeared. "That was for Natalie. And that was for Tommy. Now I can finally live with what I did."

With that, he confirmed the fear: he knew Tommy was gone, alluding to his role as the compromised "funnel" and the tragic fate of his friend.

Three Buckles Police SUV's rolled into the clearing. Chief Alvarez stepped out of the first one, his face haggard and lined with exhaustion. He was flanked by two uniformed officers, but their posture was defensive, not aggressive. An ambulance and the coroner's van pulled in behind them.

Alvarez walked slowly toward the church door, his eyes sweeping the scene—the bullet hole, Crawford's body, the stillness of the church.

Alvarez approached, his badge clipped to his belt, face drawn.

Sarah turned sharply. "You've got nerve showing up."

Alvarez didn't flinch. "I had to."

"You ignored Emilee. I was basically begging for your help."

"I wasn't ignoring you," he said quietly. "I was in Springfield. With the DOJ."

Sarah blinked. "What?"

"I needed you to think I had been compromised that I was in on it, I had to. Delaney threatened to reopen a sealed complaint—said she'd ruin me if I interfered."

Sarah stepped closer, voice low. "So, you just disappeared?"

"I knew this town didn't have the resources. No subpoena power.

No protection. I needed federal backing. I needed to build the case without tipping them off."

He looked past her, toward Crawford's body.

"I didn't know it would end like this. I thought I had time."

Sarah's voice cracked. "You didn't."

Alvarez nodded. "I know. That's why I'm here now. No more silence."

He handed her a flash drive.

"Everything I've got. Sticker logs. altered charts. Internal memos. It's all there."

Sarah stared at it. Then at him.

"You better be ready to testify."

Alvarez met her gaze. "I've been ready. I just needed someone who'd listen."

"Welcome back from the dark side," she said.

Alvarez gave a tired smile. "Had to take a walk through the shadows to see what was hiding there."

She nodded. "You remember those stories we told? The drunk under the streetlight. The mouse in the cream."

He chuckled. "Hard to forget."

"Well," Sarah said, stepping beside him, "this time, two mice were drowning in cream. The first one tried to give up. The second one prayed the cream would turn to beer."

Alvarez raised an eyebrow.

"And then," she continued, "a drunk came along, drank the beer, the mice climbed out, found the keys, and drove off."

Alvarez laughed, a real laugh, the kind that cracked through months of tension.

Sarah grinned. "Moral of the story? Sometimes being underestimated is the best fuel. You were wrong about me—but it pushed me harder. And you're here now. That's what matters."

Alvarez nodded. "Guess I'm riding shotgun."

Sarah quips "Just don't touch the radio."

He smirked and looked toward the officers and waved them forward. "Secure the scene. Lock down the exits. This whole damn place is now evidence."

Marcus followed, limping, but halfway across the floor, he stopped. His knees buckled, and he sank to the ground. They gave him space. He needed it.

Sarah turned to Alvarez, pulling the folder with the blueprints and records from her bag. "It's all here," she said. "The tunnels. The records. The victims."

Alvarez took the folder, flipped through the pages, then looked up and nodded. "The DOJ's on the way, It's out of your hands now."

She smiled

Marcus stood at the window, staring out into the trees. His posture was rigid, but his mind was far away. Beyond the glass, the woods pulsed with quiet life. Hayes didn't flinch at the sound of approaching engines.

He touched the tattoo hidden under his sleeve—a faded Brahma bull. It was old, inked before the war, before everything changed.

He looked at Sarah, then at the chaos around them.

His voice was quiet, but steady.

"I used to say, 'Trust no one but yourself.'"

He exhaled.

"But that's how they win. That's how they keep us isolated.

Truth needs allies. And I'm done being alone."

He turned again to the window, staring out into the trees. The clearing was still; the sky with the sun peering behind shadows. Mist clung low to the ground like breath held too long. Then, from the edge of the woods, three deer emerged—thin, slow-moving, their ribs visible beneath patchy coats.

They stepped into the clearing with the same eerie calm as before, hooves silent on the frost-hardened grass. One lifted its head, ears twitching, and looked straight at him through the glass.

Unblinking. Unafraid.

They looked like **ghost**s—like something the land had tried to forget but couldn't quite bury.

Marcus didn't move.

Then came the sound.

A low rumble. Tires on gravel.

The deer startled, bolted—vanishing into the trees just as the first black SUV crested the hill.

Outside, the sirens crescendoed. Black SUVs rolled into the clearing. Department of Justice agents stepped out—flashlights in hand, expressions unreadable.

Sarah helped Emilee to her feet. "Let's get you checked out," she stated.

Near the pulpit, two medics crouched beside Crawford's body. The coroner snapped a photo of the cooler seal, then logged the time: 17:33. Chain of custody began the moment the body stopped breathing. Crawford's organs were viable.

The coroner looked up. "Protocol doesn't discriminate. Get the perfusion kit."

Sarah paused, watching from a distance. Emilee leaned against her. "They're treating him like cargo," Sarah whispered.

Emilee's voice was hoarse. "That's what he taught them."

CHAPTER 48 – FALLOUT

The motel room was quiet, lit by soft morning light filtering through the blinds. Sarah lay in bed, propped against a pillow, her legal pad still open beside her. Her eyes were tired but alert, scanning the ceiling like it might offer answers.

Marcus entered with two coffees, one in each hand. He set hers on the nightstand without a word, then sat at the edge of the bed.

Sarah reached for the remote and turned on the TV. The screen lit up with a live broadcast—muted. Protesters outside Trinity General. A scrolling headline: *Federal Agents Raid Hospital in Rockford County Scandal.*

She didn't look at the screen. She picked up the newspaper instead.

Sarah's eyes scanned the next headline, bold and unflinching:

The front page bore the headline:

Buried Beneath Rockford County: A Town's Medical Secrets Unearthed *Special Investigation by Scott Washman*

She read in silence.

"What began as whispers in a veterans shelter has erupted into one of the most disturbing medical scandals in Missouri history. Detective Sarah Hart, whose notes and firsthand accounts have now been turned over to federal authorities, exposed a network of underground corridors connecting key institutions—Trinity General Hospital , the courthouse, and more. These conduits, she alleges, were used to traffic vulnerable individuals: patients, runaways, and the undocumented."

"Records show a pattern of overmedication, falsified diagnoses, and unexplained deaths. Antibiotics were used to mask symptoms and preserve organs. Consent forms were forged, bodies were moved without family notification, and in at least one case, a warehouse was used as a temporary holding site for victims awaiting transport."

"Dr. Anika Shah, a former transplant ethicist, had warned the board two years ago. 'You're not saving lives,' she'd said. 'You're laundering death.' Her contract was terminated within the week, she wasn't seen again."

"Federal agents arrived on scene early yesterday morning. A survivor—a nurse at Trinity General Hospital —was recovered and is now under medical care. The Department of Justice has confirmed sealed indictments, grand jury convening, and federal RICO implications. Evelyn Harrow was seen leaving the courthouse after being subpoenaed to testify as a former donor."

"In the hours following the broadcast, a wave of anonymous blogs and social media accounts surfaced, all aimed at discrediting Detective Hart. The language was coordinated, the accusations recycled—claims of misconduct, instability, and bias but, none of it held. The evidence she provided was airtight, and the federal response swift."

"A confidential internal fundraising memo written by Dr. Crawford—disguised as spiritual guidance—was also recovered. It stated: 'While the world focuses on the chaos of the waiting list, we, the Chosen, must maintain focus on the purity of the Yield. Our mission is not merely triage, but to ensure that the lives of the deserving are extended by the Sacrifice of the forgotten. Every dollar donated moves us closer to achieving God's perfect Order.'"

When Detective Hart was asked about it, she stated:

"I'm not here to speculate. I'm here to testify. I saw the conduits. I saw the silence that let it happen."

Marcus turns up the TV

"Federal Lawsuit Filed Against Trinity General: Widow Alleges Medical Battery, Fraud, and Intentional Harm"

"Filed in Rockford County Circuit Court just hours before federal agents descended on Trinity General, the civil suit —brought by a woman identified only as *Mrs. X*—alleges a pattern of deliberate medical misconduct leading to the death of her husband, Mr. X. The complaint outlines a chilling sequence of events: the administration of unnecessary medications, the administration of insulin, the use of sedatives and antipsychotics without psychiatric indication, and the unauthorized delivery of a flu vaccine and ocular preservatives —standard in donor preparation protocols."

"The suit claims Mr. X was not suffering from the infections Trinity cited in his death summary. Instead, he was in acute heart failure, with a dangerously low ejection fraction. Despite this, he was subjected to a pharmacological regimen that, according to the suit, 'mirrored known organ preservation strategies rather than therapeutic care.'"

"The complaint further alleges that Trinity General falsified medical records, altered portal logs, and issued a postmortem summary that contradicted earlier documentation. When Mrs. X requested an independent review, she received what her legal team describes as 'a condescending dismissal and a retroactively edited chart.'"

"The lawsuit names Trinity General Hospital , several attending physicians, and former administrator Evelyn Harrow as defendants. It seeks damages for wrongful death, medical battery, fraud, and emotional distress, and calls for a federal investigation into what it terms 'a systemic pattern of covert donor targeting and concealment.'"

Pan live to the chief, Chief Alvarez's voice filled the room…

Sarah folded the paper slowly and set it aside.

"Books like *Chosen Vessels: The Burden of Spiritual Authority* confirm Dr. Crawford was operating under a messianic delusion. This wasn't just about profit—it was doctrine."

A reporter called out, "Is it true Dr. Crawford said, 'I was helping people! They were dying anyway'?"

Alvarez shook his head. "I can't speak to that."

Another reporter asked, "Is this over?"

Alvarez glanced to his right—barely off camera stood a balding man in khaki pants, glasses, and a comb-over. The camera zoomed in slightly making the man out of view as Alvarez continued:

"This isn't just about one hospital ," the lead agent stated. "It's a network—and we're going to dismantle it. The Department of Justice agents did a sweep through Trinity General Hospital . They seized files and documented the holding rooms."

Sarah leaned back in her seat, eyes on the chaos.

"Who was that?" she asked, referring to the man behind Alvarez.

Marcus stood behind her, watching too. "I didn't see him," he said. "But what I do know is—this is just the beginning."

He sat beside her. He didn't smile, but his eyes softened.

"We're not done," he said. "Not until the whole system falls."

Then Marcus leaned in and kissed her forehead.

"I'll be back soon."

Sarah looked at him—flat, knowing. "Yeah, right."

He smiled faintly.

"Go do what you need to," she said. "I'll be here."

Three days later, Sarah stepped into the motel lobby, her badge clipped to her belt, her coat slung over one arm.

The town was split. Some called her a hero. Others called her a liar. Trinity General Hospital 's board released a statement denying everything.

"Ms. Hart?" the clerk called gently. "These were left for you."

He held out a bouquet of wildflowers—fresh, bright, slightly uneven.

Sarah took them without speaking.

Back in her room, she laid her coat and keys on the desk. The flowers sat in her hands a moment longer before she spotted the envelope tucked between the stems.

She opened the card.

They're moving the rest. Tonight. Tunnel 3. —M. H.

Her breath caught.

She thought, "They raided the building but, the system? The system's still breathing"

She grabbed her coat, her keys, a flashlight, and her notebook—

and ran out the door.

CHAPTER 49 - BONUS CHAPTER – THE TWIST

The shower hissed behind her, steam curling into the corners of the room. Sarah sat on the edge of the bed, one leg tucked under the other, her notebook open but untouched.

Marcus was singing softly—off-key, something bluesy. She smiled. He only sang when he thought no one was listening.

Her eyes drifted across the room. His duffel bag slouched in the corner; the initials stitched into the canvas: M.H. His watch lay on the nightstand, flipped over, the engraving catching the light: M.H. A note still pinned to the fridge from last week: *"Ran to the store—okay, I didn't run, lol. I'll be back, beautiful ❤ —M.H."*

She stared at the letters. M.H.

Her mind flicked back to the charts. The stickers. The codes. S.M.H.

She remembered the envelope Marcus had handed her weeks ago —documents, scribbled notes, a list of names. On the front, he'd written: S: J.T. She'd asked what the "S" meant. He'd said, *"Sent. That's how I track who I pass things to. Keeps the chain clean."*

She hadn't thought much of it then but, now...

She remembered Marcus once saying, "Natalie wasn't just my wife. She was my partner."

The water stopped. Silence.

Sarah stood, walked to the bathroom door, and knocked once. "Hey?"

Marcus's voice came through, low and steady. "Yeah?"

She pushed the door open just as he stepped out, towel around his waist, water dripping from his hair. He leaned in and kissed her.

She pushed him back playfully. "Wait a second there, tiger. I've got a question."

He raised an eyebrow. "This sounds serious."

"You promised never to lie to me, right?"

"Right."

"Okay. What does SMH mean?"

Marcus blinked. "You're asking me this now?"

She nodded. "Does it mean 'Sent to Marcus Hayes'?"

He looked around the room. His eyes landed on the duffel bag. The watch. The note.

He sighed. "Okay. So, this is the conversation we're about to have, huh?"

He walked over, pulled on his pants, then moved to the kitchenette. He poured two cups of coffee, handed one to her, and sat down across from her.

Sarah didn't wait. "I'm just going to come right out with what I think to make it easier on you, okay?"

Marcus gave a slow nod.

"I think S.M.H means sent to Marcus Hayes. I think you work for the DOJ. I think you're a deep operative. I think Natalie was your partner and her cover was as your wife. I think SMH was put on items that were sent to you—to remind the person you had on the inside what was sent and what wasn't. I think that person was Natalie, until she disappeared. So, you came in as her upset husband looking for his missing wife, when the reality is she's still around somewhere, helping from behind the mirror. And you played homeless to find Roy."

Marcus stared at her for a long moment. Then he said, "Okay. First of all—Natalie and I were married. That wasn't a cover. And she's not behind any mirrors. Crawford confirmed that."

Sarah's voice softened. "Then how did you get me involved in this case?"

"I didn't," Marcus said. "Tommy's sister calling about him—that was all real but, once I saw you in action, saw how you were… yeah, I thought you could get a lot further than I was. That's why I didn't come to see you until that night at the shelter."

Sarah nodded slowly. "And Emilee turning hospital evidence?"

"Organic," Marcus said. "I never saw that one coming. I thought I had my guy."

"Your guy?" Sarah asked. She thought back. Her eyes widened. "No… don't tell me it was Grady."

They both laughed.

"Wait…" she said, narrowing her eyes. "Delaney's assistant, Spencer?"

Marcus sipped his coffee, eyes just visible above the rim of the cup.

He winked.

There was a knock at the door.

"Are you freakin' kidding me," Sarah whispered. "Timing. Timing is everything—oh my Lord."

She walked to the door and peeked through the peephole. "Oh man. She's lucky it's her."

She opened the door. There stood Nurse Emilee Vaughn.

"Get in here," Sarah said, grabbing her into a hug. Emilee buried her face in Sarah's shoulder.

Marcus got up and walked over. Sarah let go, and Emilee turned. Marcus opened his arms, and Emilee hugged him with everything she had.

They all had tears of joy in their eyes.

"You look cleaner. Calmer," Sarah half-joked.

Marcus interrupted, "You're carrying the quiet resolve of a survivor."

They all sat down—Sarah and Marcus on one bed, Emilee across from them on the other.

Emilee held something small and silver in her hand: Marcus's broken necklace chain, complete with the dog tags and Natalie's silver cross.

"You lost something," Emilee said softly, placing the broken chain gently between them on the nightstand. "I found it right where the tunnels split into the warehouse."

Marcus looked at the cross—the key, the evidence, the object of a decade of pain, now returned to him covered in grime and shadow. He had been chasing it his entire adult life.

He looked up at Sarah. Her steady strength, the stubborn loyalty, the fight that had survived a sedative attack and political betrayal. He could see the future he hadn't dared to claim.

He gently picked up the chain. "No," he corrected, his voice thick. "I gained something."

He separated the cross from the dog tags, leaving the military past on the table. He leaned toward Sarah and gently clasped the cross around her neck.

"Natalie's fight is over," he whispered, his eyes meeting hers. "Her hope isn't. Keep it, Sarah. Let it be the symbol of the truth you held, and the faith I have in you to keep fighting the system. Maybe, for the first time, I can have faith in the system, too—because you're still standing in it."

Sarah touched the cool, worn silver. Her gaze was steady, accepting the weight of the cross and the hope it now represented. She was no longer just a detective fighting a lost cause; she was the keeper of a sacrifice.

Outside, the heavy cloud cover parted to bright sun, rays beaming over the county. The investigations were far from over. New battles lay ahead—in courtrooms, in Congress, and in the political shadows but, they all knew one thing with absolute certainty: they weren't alone in the fight.

(As the scene fades, talk radio hums in the background):

"Buckles thrives on contradiction. It sells faith and fantasy, humility and spectacle. Behind the scenes, the town runs on seasonal labor, tight margins, and quiet understandings. Locals know the rhythm: spring brings the motor coaches, summer the crowds, fall the gospel festivals. Winter? That's for repairs, rumors… and reckoning."

2 months later -

The courthouses air hovered with scents of old paper and lemon polish—clean enough to pretend. Judge Delaney's portrait still hung above the juvenile intake desk; eyes fixed on the hallway where children disappeared into custody. The raid had made headlines. The indictments hadn't. And somewhere in the basement, a clerk stamped "Handled" on a file that didn't exist last week...

(to be continued...)

NO MORE SILENCE

Reform must happen: pharmaceutical kickbacks must end; patient-to-doctor ratios must be reduced; the revolving door of physicians treating a single patient must close; there must be external oversight, external patient advocates that stay with the patient when family cant, external performance reviews, mandatory education on non-pharmaceutical, remedies; organ donation protocols must be rewritten; and the altering or falsifying of medical records must carry heavy criminal punishment.

"They isolated us, degraded us, ignored us, and ultimately silenced us. Silence is the fuel institutions like this depend on to carry on with their conceited corruption and exploitation. My loss created a momentum that developed a voice—and that voice will speak until reform is no longer a plea, but a reality, that voice will not stop until change is no longer optional, but inevitable." - T.R. Richardson

EXTRAS

SORTING FLOWCHART

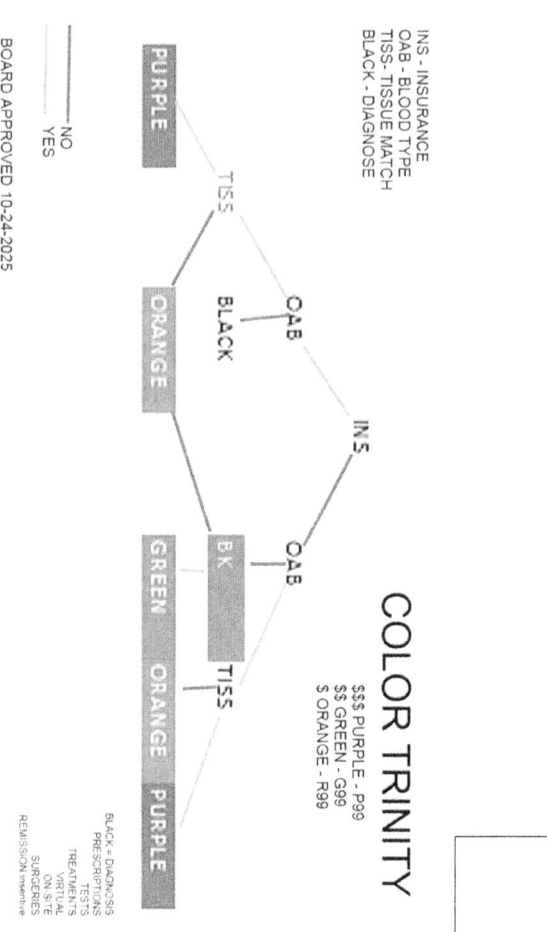

Made in the USA
Coppell, TX
17 January 2026

69453630R00134